FATE KISSED

PHOENIX RISING BOOK THREE

ANNIE ANDERSON

This book is dedicated to all those who live with regret. It is not too late to change it, my dear. Your time is not up. The last of your breath has not passed your lips. You are still alive.

PROLOGUE

EVAN—1906—SAN FRANCISCO, CA

IN THIS SEA OF RUBBLE AND FLAMES, I WISH I COULD remember why I was so angry, but I seem to have forgotten. I vaguely remember the danger and rage that provoked me, but at this very moment, I cannot fathom how I let it get this far.

What I do know is that I caused this mess, and the longer I look around, the longer I hear the screams of the trapped and dying over the ringing in my ears; the more I know I should let the flames consume me.

I feel the souls, so many souls out there, and most of them were good people.

And I killed them all.

My gaze focuses on a broken baby doll, the pale

china face half gone, crumbled to dust in the melee of toppling buildings and shaking earth. A lone child's slipper rests in the middle of the cracked street, teetering on the edge of the broken brick, waffling between the coming fire and oblivion.

The flames creep lazily toward me, tip-toeing their way across the buildings as if they have all the time in the world to put me out of my misery, to dole out my punishment.

I deserve this. I deserve to burn.

I have failed my parents, my race, and for the life of me, I cannot remember why. How could I do this?

Suddenly, it all comes rushing through the fog of shock and the thick ringing in my ears.

Men came in the night. They came for me—for my head—and the poor souls who called themselves my Guardians lost theirs instead. I can still see the shocked look on Devereux's face when the blade pierced his neck, his wide eyes are burned into my brain as if with a hot iron.

I don't think he ever expected them to get this far. To follow us all the way across the country to the bustling port of San Francisco. He thought we were safe in the throng of people coming and going.

He was wrong.

Now, Devereux and Sam are both gone, cut down

like wheat against the scythe, and I have no idea what to do. Guilt claws at me, sharp and bleeding.

I didn't mean to lose my mind. I didn't mean to reap this much death.

But I had no idea I was this powerful. I had no idea I could cause so much destruction.

The city is in ruins, like a dollhouse thrown by a toddler in a fit of rage. And what is worse is I am so hungry, starving for the stained souls calling for me to send them to Hell. My fangs descend, cutting into my lips and bringing the coppery taste of blood to my tongue. It only makes me hungrier, and I fight my body's urge to travel to them, to glut myself on the souls of the evil.

I can't do it. I can't send them to Hell when I deserve to go myself. Closing my eyes to the mayhem, I wait for the flames to do their duty.

"Are you going to get out of the way or are you planning on burning to death?" a husky female's voice calls to me.

I blink through my haze of shock to see a woman not much bigger than my own meager height eyeing me like I was a bug on her boot. And her eyes... No pupil and such a pale milky green, she shouldn't be able to see me, but by the expression on her face, she most certainly does.

Dressed as a man in trousers and a waistcoat, she has to be the oddest person I've ever encountered. And for a Wraith in the middle of a ruined city, that's saying something.

"No offense, girlie, but Wraiths like you tend to fry when exposed to open flame. You might want to move," she says matter-of-factly, and that's when I lose it.

"I-I...did this. C-caused all this," I stutter as my breaths come in great gasping heaves, and I break right there in the middle of the cracked street.

Then, the bricks start abrading away underneath my feet, and I feel the pull of the silence, the deadness in my own head calling for me to put it all away. The guilt, the fear, the pain of losing my closest friends—all of it.

I don't see the fist coming for my face until it's too late, and before I know what hits me, blackness clouds my mind.

I wanted oblivion, I think as the lights fade out. It might not be the death I asked for, but a nice sleep will do.

Yes, it will do just fine.

I

WEST

One would think people would know by now, but they don't. People as a whole are dumb, lazy bastards only out for themselves. Plenty would like to think they're different, but having nearly six hundred years of experience in the selfishness of people, I can attest they're all the same.

Maybe it's just Wraiths that are like this. Perhaps the other factions see us as the cockroaches of the Ethereal because of the way we act. Or maybe it's because of who we are as the gateways to Hell, the soul-eaters of the damned...

It's probably a bit of both.

Welcome to the Ethereal! Where we don't give a shit

what color you are, but if you have powers we don't like, well, then fuck you.

I silently chuckle a little to myself. Yep, the game show host in my head has definitely lost his nut. It's easier to stave off the grief if I make myself laugh, but I know my good humor won't last for long.

My King is dead, my Queen along with him. And the mantle I've kept—the vow I took—is a hard thing to let go of.

Even if I have been released. Dismissed. Fired. Whatever.

The job isn't finished and fired or not, I'm still going to make sure it gets done.

Staying in the shadows—not too hard up here on the cliff top across the gorge from John and Olivia's home—I crouch in the darkness of a yawning crevasse. But it isn't their home any longer, is it? They're gone now, death taking them one after the other and all too soon.

I spy the Wraiths in fancy funeral dresses and tuxes prepare to fight a battle they can't win, a few hauling long-range precision rifles from narrow, padded gun cases.

I guess they aren't messing around anymore, but what I really want to know is who in the hell starts a fight at funeral?

The group is dressed very differently from me. While they look refined and out of place as they spoil for a fight, I look right at home with the prospect of a good, old fashioned blood bath in my black fighting leathers and body armor.

Luck favors the prepared, so the saying goes, and I am very, very lucky.

Smoking out from the cliff top, I travel to a nook on the roof of the house overlooking the gorge where I think Ian might be hiding. Ian possesses an innate ability, making him almost impossible to find if he decides to cloak himself. It pisses me off that I've never been able to find him.

"You looking for me?" Ian asks as he appears in front of me as if from thin air. One second there was nothing, and the next he's lying prone on the rooftop looking through the scope of a fifty-caliber sniper rifle, his dark skin midnight in the moonlight.

I've been looking all over this roof for the last ten minutes, and he's been there the whole damn time. *Dick.*

"Are sure you're not half-witch instead of half-human?" I ask, my voice gruff from disuse. I haven't spoken in the last day—not that I speak much to anyone but Evan...

Or, at least, I did. My girl could talk your ear off, and

I'd never tell her, but I love her chatter, her life. She kept me from sliding into the darkness.

Now I have nothing to keep me from darkest parts of my soul.

She is air and light... I miss my light. I miss my Angel.

"Who knows? Dad got around," he quips as he adjusts the elevation dial on his scope.

It pulls me back into the moment, his tone laced with just a hint of derision, and it dawns on me that the circumstances of his birth might be a sore subject.

Oops.

I study his rifle with dubious interest. I have an issue with long-range weapons as a whole. If I'm doing the job, I'm doing it right, and it's too hard to do a dead check from a thousand yards away. None of this 'from afar' bullshit. But it's harder to kill me than it is Ian.

I suppose we must go with our strengths, and the up-close kill is mine.

"Are you going to be able to stay cloaked and fire at the same time?" I ask because he's no good here if he can't.

"Yep. The only thing I can't hide is the sound, but the echo from the mountains will cover it for me. No one will know where I am unless they're right next to me, and even then, they won't live long enough to do anything about it," he murmurs as he adjusts the elevation dial again.

"Good. I'll handle the shitheads on the cliff. You handle any that get too close to the family," I order, and I want to kick myself.

Again.

I don't lead him anymore. I'm not in charge of anyone's security, let alone Evangeline's. My chest aches from her loss. Well, and the fact that my skin is still growing back from her blistering shove. I rub my hand over my sternum, only hurting myself more when I hit body armor.

Pissing her off wasn't part of the plan. Hurting her is the absolute last thing I ever wanted to do. Guess I should have told her why. Why I was waiting to claim her. Not because of her—never because of her.

But who really accepts the 'it's not you, it's me' shit? That's right. No one.

I should have told her all of it, should have made her understand. I hope I'll live long enough to do just that.

"Will do," he says as he pulls his eye from the scope and grins at my gaff.

Ian has hope. Hope I'll come back and everything will be as it was. I guess I still have hope, too.

"You think they'll actually do it? Start this fight?" he asks, showing his youth.

He's been on the right side for so long, he's forgotten how the other side thinks. I give him a long look telling him everything he needs to know. Yes. They will start this war, maybe not today or tomorrow, but...

War is coming.

I don't want this for her, don't want this darkness in her light.

Feeling it clawing at my back, the worry chokes my throat. The worry for Evangeline. The burden for all we have built and the peace we have so tentatively held onto. It is coming to an end, and I can kill and slash and fight, but I can't protect her like I used to. I can't be there every second.

And it's my own fault.

Trying and failing to swallow against the lump of bitter guilt, I escaping the roof, traveling back to a hidden crevasse. Waiting for the beginning of this little war.

It is almost unbearable to watch Evangeline tear up as she sent her parents on, and even worse, I can't hear her voice from up here. More so, I wasn't there with them to send my friends—my family—to their peace.

My chest burns again, but I refuse to rub away the ache. Instead, I ball my fists, cracking my knuckles in the process, and get ready for the shit to hit the fan.

I've tested my weapons more than once, making

sure the blades are sharp, my armor is secure. I don't need to go through it all again, but my hands ache to do something. I can't stand another moment of inaction. I adjust my favorite ivory-hilted Kukris, the blades secured in an inverted holster crisscrossed behind my back.

I have never been one to lie in wait. Usually, when people are sent to me, it is because they needed killing. More often than not, the people who needed killing, needed it done to send a message. As the King's assassin, I kept the peace. Killing here and there with almost surgical precision to stamp out threats. But delicacy is not my forte.

I understand why I need to wait for them to make the first move—sniper rifles and all –even if I don't like it. If this group of stupid soon-to-be-dead fucks decides the fight's not worth it, I can't just rip into them—no matter how much I want to. I have to have a reason... even if that reason might blow my whole plan to Hell and back.

It isn't long before they give me one.

Three men ruin their fancy tuxes as they lie in the dirt to line up their shots. Time to move. Using the skills I honed early in my childhood, I make my way slowly but surely through the throng, picking off the outliers like a big cat stalking prey.

To call my past dysfunctional is like slapping a coat of paint on a condemned house. Using a pretty word won't make it any better.

Hell, dysfunctional would be a step up. Then again, anything would be a step up from where I came from.

The first ones give me no trouble, quickly snuffing out the flames of their lives with my knife. I suppose it's hard to hear me over the sound of the rifle or, perhaps, no one expected there to be a real fight at a funeral.

No one notices when the early ones go, poor bastards, and I move on to the shitheads that are doing the actual harm. Popping in and out like a ghost, I steal them away before their buddies even know what hit them. I don't bother to consume them now; I'll wait until I'm done for that. I'll glut myself on their souls, but only when I'm done.

The next round is slightly more tiresome than the first. I guess when most of your friends are missing, you start to notice, but really, how effective can you be in a tuxedo?

My cockiness bites me in the ass, then, when a little weasel in an expensive suit stabs me in the back. He misjudges my armor and hits Kevlar instead of the lung he was aiming for, the bastard. Slashing again, he hits my forearm as I go to block him, but he doesn't get to keep his weapon. I snatch it from him as easily as if I was taking it from a child.

He appears apologetic, and he's so young, I'd probably let him live if it weren't for the blood running down my back.

The dark side starts their recruiting early, I see.

I kill him quickly, painlessly, and it hurts me to do so. I hate killing the young ones—the ones just barely past maturity. While not the worst soul I've ever seen, he still had time to turn it around. If he weren't on the wrong side of a war, he would have had all the time in the world.

This will just have to be another score on my soul added to the mountain of scars from a past I can't change. Really, what's one more?

In that second of self-pity, I lose my grip on the upper hand. Three men attack me at once, stabbing and slicing with their talons like a pack of raptors. Fear trickles into my brain, and I try to beat it back, but...

It's funny, but I'm not afraid of death. Not for death or Hell. In this life, I did what I did, and I can't change it. I always did what I thought was right, and if it makes me evil, then so be it.

No, the fear I feel is for her, my Angel. My Evangeline. Because she deserves so much better in this life than this. Than me.

It is not to say I don't fight back. I do.

With every breath in me, I fight.

For her. For her smile and laugh and light. I fight. To my very last breath, I will, and even when I die, I'll fight some more.

As I dirty my soul, taking more and more life, killing the men who try to snuff out my flame, the thunder of the fifty-cal makes its presence known, earning me precious seconds that will save my hide.

I stab. I slash. I kill, and as I rip my blade against the last throat of the last of what is left of the Wraiths on top of the cliff, I feel a warring sense of disgust for myself and a little satisfaction at a job well done.

No one saw me. I was sure of it. Well, no one who could live to tell the tale, anyway. It is the satisfaction that kills me a little more each day. I shouldn't be proud of this. I shouldn't feel a sense of accomplishment at stomping out life.

Even if the souls I took were on the expressway straight to Hell. And they were, believe me. I don't kill innocents.

Never again, you mean, my mind snidely whispers, reminding me of mistakes from a previous life.

I look over the edge of the cliff at the gritty, rocky shore of the river, and feel the cold slap of regret.

I'm an asshole. A lousy good-for-nothing steaming pile of shit.

I know this.

But I didn't think she did until I see her face scanning the blackness for me in the dark of the gorge.

I should have shown my face, should have fought beside her instead of taking out the men from the shadows.

But it would blow my cover, and before I can fix what I broke by eliminating the threat to her life, I'll have to walk right into the snake pit.

And those slimy bastards don't need to know my only weakness.

Her.

2

EVAN

I'm livid. This isn't a new thing for me. Lately, I get angry at the drop of a hat. It's no surprise, I mean come on. Who wouldn't be mad? I'd figure today of all days I would get to just be sad.

I put my parents to rest today. I should be crying into a big glass of bourbon right about now.

Nope, not me.

Instead, on the first day of my rule, I not only had to fight for my life, but I also had to *fight to fight* for my life. I was treated like a child by the very men I'm supposed to lead. Sure, I killed the men who conspired to murder my parents in probably the worst way I can think of, but in the grand scheme, I didn't get the head of the snake. I don't even know who the snake *is*.

That will have to come later.

And then I have Idiot One and Idiot Two trying to keep me from fighting alongside my family.

I don't think so.

I take a look around at the aftermath of the gorge. Other than some scorched rock, one would never know so many lost their lives here. In the silence, now that the guns have spent their rounds and the weapons have all been sheathed, the only sound apart from the rush of the water over the rock is the faint beat of Mena's wings as she searches for another threat.

She won't find one.

Wraiths rarely fight if they think they can't win. This is why we've lived in 'peace' for so many years. Why start a war when you can just kill someone in the dead of night and blame somebody else?

Wraith logic. We are a sunny bunch, aren't we?

Mena circles once, twice, and then finally lands on a large boulder jutting into the water from the shore. Phasing almost immediately, she jumps from the rock into Asher's arms, and a new ache wrenches in my chest. *West.*

He didn't come, didn't stay. He didn't help.

The ragged edges of my heart start bleeding once

again. I know I released him. I know I told him I never wanted to see him again, and it's true—I don't. Not really, despite the pitiful whining of my heart. I couldn't keep relying on someone who was never going to choose me—who was never going to stay with me.

I can barely wrap my mind around the fact that he *knew* we were mates, knew that the Fates chose us to be together. He felt it with me and decided to deny me. For one hundred and nine years he's denied me. Turning his nose up at all we could be.

You'd think I'd know better by now.

I finally wised up, but only a little, because I was still shocked when he didn't come to the funeral. *Shocked.* How stupid can I be?

A lot, apparently, because I'm still stinging with jealousy from watching Mena and Asher, and as each beat of my heart begins to ache in my chest, I realize I just can't take one more thing today. Before I can leave, my best friend in the entire universe grabs my hand. I'm not looking at her, but I know it's Aurelia. The pain in my chest eases for a moment, and I have never been more glad she is here with me.

Saving me from the fire from the very first day we met, Aurelia knows me better than anyone—even if I've been keeping huge secrets from her.

Pulling me close, she wraps her arms around me, the natural heat of her skin warming me.

"I'll only be able to stall them for a few minutes so you can get your shit together, but *only* a few minutes. The house is empty, so use your time wisely," she whispers into my ear before giving me another squeeze.

I can work with a few minutes. That is just enough time to sling back a shot of bourbon and get out of this stupid gown. Who decided to make funerals formal attire only, for pity's sake?

Not taking the time to ponder the origins of Wraith customs, I travel from the multicolored rock floor of the gorge to my room in the cliff house.

It is an opulent room—far too rich for my taste— but Mama decorated it for me, and I didn't have the heart to tell her it wasn't me. Now, that she's gone, I can't imagine changing it.

The walls are papered in a lightly textured, luminescent cream. In fact, most of the room is in shades of white and silver from the wallpaper to the mirrored side tables. The only color—and my only contribution to the design of the room—is from a plush magenta area rug that is begging me to walk on it. I detour around the white leather sitting chairs just so I can walk across the soft shag on my way to the liquor nook hidden away by an antique-white paneled cabinet.

My mother and the white. *I'm not a virgin, Mama. That ship sailed a long time ago.*

I pull a squat tumbler from the lowest shelf and splash a healthy measure in the glass. I only get a single swallow in before Cam and Aidan bust my door open like an episode of Cops. They file in my room like they are my wardens, and I realize now, letting them get away with the shit they pulled in the gorge was a mistake on my part.

"Well, that was unnecessary," I say before I can stop myself, and I'm happy it comes out calm as you please instead of the seething rage bubbling in my chest.

"What the hell do you think you're doing, Evangeline?" Cam thunders, his hulking form fills the doorway, the black of his clothes making him look only more ominous.

He is chastising me like a naughty toddler.

Yep, big mistake on my part. *Sorry, Papa, I've failed you already.*

Taking another swallow of my bourbon, I carelessly fling the glass back in the cabinet. Before the tumbler can stop spinning on the bar top, I've traveled to the pair of them and have Cam face first on the tile with his hand pinned behind his back.

First my parents, then West, now this. I am already shitting the bed at this whole leader thing. I am done failing, and if there is anything I learned from my father, it was sometimes lessons need to be taught the hard way.

As my talons gouge into Cam's face, I turn my black eyes to Aidan, and by his expression, I can tell he didn't expect me to know how to fight nor did he know I could take someone much bigger than myself down.

We've fought together. He should know better.

"I assume this tantrum is because I left the gorge?" I ask, and Aidan hesitantly nods.

Cam doesn't move an inch, and I don't blame him. One wrong move and his eye is going bye-bye.

"I have some issues with your behavior at the funeral. First and foremost, you held me back from fighting," I say calmly.

"We did our job. We were keeping you safe," Aidan gently pleads and while I appreciate the sentiment, I can't abide by it.

"Would you have refused to let my father fight? Would you have tried to take that away from him?" I ask, and I can tell my question hits home.

He has undermined me without meaning to, and at the realization, Aidan's face goes white.

Aidan and Cam have been with my family long before I was born. They see me as a child, a little sister, and while I trust them with my life, I can't trust them to guard me against the dangers of this reign for another second without this lesson.

"No. You wouldn't," I scold, answering for him.

"But you..." Cam begins.

"Do. Not. Presume to tell me what I can and cannot do. I am your Queen, your leader, and you will treat me as such or I will make you regret it." I say through gritted teeth, and while I feel slightly guilty for smashing his face on the hardwood floor, it has to be done.

I love Cam, he is the big brother I never had. He has tended to more scraped knees than any grown man should, but family or not, he cannot keep playing big brother.

It will get us both killed.

"I love you both, but I will release you and get someone else if you can't get it through your thick skulls that I'm not a delicate little flower. I know how to handle myself. And if you undermine me again, I will make your release the permanent kind. Do you understand me?" I question as I retract my talons from his face and travel to my feet.

I get a reluctant nod from Cam as blood wells from the cuts in his cheek. Cam and Aidan both take a knee of supplication, and when they rise, five little ribbons of red have made their way down Cam's face.

"Good. If it makes you any feel better, I will continue my sparring sessions with Aurelia to keep my skills sharp. She's been training me for a decade already, I see no reason to change things up now," I admit to a stunned Aidan.

"West let you…" Aidan says, and his eyes widen as he trails off realizing his mistake.

Just the sound of his name slices into my chest, and I steady myself against the blow.

"West was not aware. He was my Guardian, not my father. I don't want to hear his name again. Now, no offense guys, but I need some alone time. I'm going to go drown my sorrows in some bourbon and take a bath. I want the door fixed before I get out. Oh, and if you bust in my room again, I'll cut something off of that you need. Understood?" I ask, but it isn't really a question.

They both got a freebie pass for pulling that bullshit in the gorge. I can't be that lenient again.

Walking back to the cabinet, I snag the bourbon and my glass from the bar top and head to the en suite bathroom, gently closing the door when I want to slam it. Flipping on the taps before moving to the walk-in, I pull the zipper down on my dress and slip it from my shoulders. Carefully putting it on the thick, wooden hanger, my mind finally catches up with me. Black gauzy fabric, heavy, black beading, I hate this dress. I want to burn it.

I want to rip it to shreds. This is the last thing I wore when I saw my parents for the final time.

It's tainted, infected with the bitter loss I'm trying so hard to stomp down into nothing. It's then that I let myself break a little and hug the now-cold dress to me as I crumple to the plush carpet.

I allow myself three minutes. Just three to vent some of this agony. I have to let it out now—where no one can see. I can't be weak, can't break.

Stemming the flow of the pain leaking from me, I climb to my feet and hang the dress on the rung. I can't let it go now. It was the last thing my mother picked out for me, the last thing we ever shopped for. Had I known at the time it was going to be my funeral dress, I wouldn't have ever bought it.

I reach up and straighten the strap on the hanger before running my fingers down the bodice.

Miss you, Mama.

I suck in a huge breath and let it out in a gust, shoring up my walls again and turn from the closet to turn the taps of the large clawfoot tub off. Filling the tumbler to the brim, I set it in the fancy teak bath tray spanning the width of the tub, and before I can think better of it, I plop the bottle of bourbon right next to it.

One night to grieve.

I need this time to deal with losing my parents.

Time to put on my big girl panties and rule as good or better than my father did. My father had to worry about his mate, and that guided his decisions. Some of those, I hate to say, treaded the safe path rather than the right one. He stayed safe to keep his mate alive.

I don't have one of those, and I probably never will.

Nope.

Safe is not for me.

I'll do the right thing instead.

3

WEST

I hate waiting, especially when it's for a pompous wanker like Voyt Garrison. I wouldn't even talk to the smarmy prick, but unfortunately, I need his help.

Perched on a stool in my garage in front of the most beautifully beat-up wreck of a motorcycle—a newer model Triumph Bonneville some idiot decided to neglect—I should feel at home. This is my place—my safe haven. The fact that my garage is twice the size of the cabin in front of it that I tenuously call home is a testament to how much I love it here.

It makes me wonder why I even have a house. I don't sleep there. I don't eat there. And I'm thoroughly afraid of opening the refrigerator, because who knows what's growing in it.

My cabin is just a place; my garage is home.

Two stories tall and four bays wide, the garage is a car lover's dream—slate gray epoxy floors, vaulted ceilings with pendant shop lights hanging from steel cables, coal black 24-gauge steel cabinets lining both the north and south walls, and the best car lift money can buy in the south bay. I even have a bed and a shower in the back room—everything I need under one roof.

Turning a wrench is the only time I feel at peace, but the waiting has yanked my attention so much I've lost the skin of three knuckles already. Yeah, I'll blame waiting instead of what I'm really doing—thinking of Evangeline.

Damn that woman.

I've been dancing around her forever, fighting my baser instincts to avoid tearing my fangs into the delicate column of her porcelain neck. Just thinking about that line of soft skin makes me fight against my dick getting hard. The way that line follows her slim shoulders and petite body, the full curve of her breasts and the gentle swell of her hips that I just so recently got a glimpse of.

A tiny glimpse. Then again, any time looking at her would be too short. I could look at her for the rest of my life, and it wouldn't be enough time. And those eyes—clearer than a Colorado sky and twice as blue. The way her nose scrunches into this adorable little frown when she's irritated. That mass of curly hair that my fingers ache to get tangled in.

It isn't just her body; it's also the sounds she makes. When she's eating her favorite dessert, she makes this little humming noise with every bite that goes straight to my dick. When she knows I'm getting lost in my own head, she tells a joke or tells me a crazy story about some trouble her and Aurelia have gotten into. And the singing. Her voice turns rough when she sings, all bluesy in a way I'd never think her normally soprano vocal cords could go.

Damn, I miss her.

Just as I think that thought, the wrench in my hands slips off the bolt, and I have another skinned knuckle. I can't keep getting distracted like this, or my own brain is going to get me killed.

And with that pleasant thought, the wrench slips again.

Motherfucking, son of a whore.

"Nice mouth, Carmichael," a voice calls drolly from the shadows of my garage.

Voyt.

Took him long enough. I had no idea I was speaking

aloud, but trust Voyt Garrison to point it out. He saunters into the light of my shop lamp, running a reverent finger over the fender of my fully restored 1950 Chevy ICON Thriftmaster. I did everything on the pickup except for the painting. The fact that he's touching it makes my lips pull into a snarl. First my girl, now my truck. If he keeps thirsting after what's mine, I'm going to rip his arms off.

"What took you so long? Needed to change your shorts after Evangeline got through with you?" I taunt, and I'm asshole enough to enjoy the uncomfortable twist to his face before he can mask it.

"Wouldn't you have?" he asks, and it is so self-deprecating, I have to give him that point.

"Eh… Probably," I chuckle tossing the wrench close to its proper spot.

Evangeline organized them all years ago, labeling the spots with her trusty label maker. She used specialty glue so the labels would stick to the foam insert. I can't even look at my own tools without missing her.

"So you wanted me here, and against my better judgment, I agreed. What do you need, West? Because this cloak and dagger crap isn't really my forte," he grumbles pulling my gaze from the stupid foam back to him.

"There was an attempt on Evangeline's life tonight,"

I say dropping a massive bomb on the likely clueless Voyt.

"What?" he growls his eyes going from green to the black of a phase so quick, even I'm surprised.

"Don't you worry your gelled little locks about it, I made sure none of the bastards lived. But they didn't think this shit up on their own. They looked more like pawns. I think some of the head families are behind it—it is the only thing that makes sense to me. They have to be responsible for John and Olivia's deaths, and that cannot stand," I inform him, and if anything it just brings an even more crazed look to his eyes.

His fingers rip through his perfectly coiffed, expertly gelled hair as a snarl erupts from his throat.

"You're telling me after I watched my two best men get liquefied right in front of my eyes, more death happened?" he asks on a demand as he starts pacing in front of the truck.

"What you mean to say is, after Evangeline's parents were poisoned and killed, several members of our community tried to murder her. Because if you say that you are upset you lost those two assholes, I'm going to rip your dick off," I growl, barely staving off the right hook I so desperately want to plant in his temple.

"No, I do not lament the loss of two duplicitous men whom I obviously had no idea could... Our species as a whole is dwindling into nothing, you idiot. We had maybe ten thousand Wraiths left in the *world* after the Phoenix attacks, and now... There should be millions of us to keep the balance. To send the souls to Hell for good instead of them just sitting in rotting corpses waiting for some witch or warlock or shapeshifter to steal the energy and start some real trouble. There are too many souls for us to reap and not enough of us to go around. And we just lost more," he rants, still pacing in a jerky clip.

"So, you're worried about the hypothetical instead of the shit we're swimming in now?"

"No. I'm worried about how many I'm going to have to kill to keep her alive. I am well aware you don't care how many you kill, but *I* do," he insists pointing to his chest as he does so.

Trust Voyt to know where to hit to cause the most damage. The scars of the people I've killed are not healed on my soul. Rather, they are big gaping wounds that refuse to mend. But I don't kill without reason, and I don't kill the innocent.

Never again.

"I don't kill innocents, Voyt. Even the King's assassin has scruples," I growl.

"Of course not," he mutters, his tone scathing. "What exactly do you need from me?"

"I need an in with the Emerson family. If there were a head family that had anything to do with this, it would be them."

They are also the only head family that was conspicuously absent from the funeral, but I don't say that.

"And why is that? The Emersons have been one of the most upstanding families—they have helped so much with the aftermath of the attacks," Voyt says in disbelief.

Helped, my ass. I've never seen a family more two-faced.

"Devereux and Sampson Emerson were Evangeline's Guardians before me. They were killed in their service. If there is any family that has a serious grudge against her, it would be them," I inform him, and the hope on his face dies replaced with dawning horror.

"*Fates*," he mutters like a curse, and it is the first time Voyt and I have ever agreed on anything.

"I'm not going to attack anyone, but it would be much easier to suss out who the culprits are if I have an in with them. I may not be Evangeline's Guardian anymore, but that doesn't mean my job is done."

Voyt's eyes go wide in shock as he takes a step back. "She released you?"

"Don't sound so broken up about it, asshole. She's my mate, and I love her more than anything. But I... I can't bind her. Not yet. Not until I know she's safe. I'm trying to keep her safe," I admit, and it burns me to do so.

This isn't about avoiding the monarchy, it is about keeping her alive. As the King's Assassin, I made enemies. There are people out there who would rather see me as maggot food than to take another breath. I can't tie her life to mine for so many reasons, but the fact that I have a huge target on my back is at the top of the list.

"And she released you because you won't bind her," he guesses offhandedly.

"Got it in one."

"I assume you have a good reason for not binding her," he whispers, his voice has turned deadly.

He cares for her, and as much as it kills me to ask him for a favor, he is probably the only person I can trust to help me and keep her safe. Granted his reasons make me want to rip his arms off, but... if he keeps her safe, I have to respect him.

Voyt's face closes down, and I can no longer get a bead on him. From a man with my considerable people-reading skills, the thought of not being able to gauge him freaks me a bit. He is silent for a few moments but continues his pacing before he stops suddenly, breathes a huge sigh of resignation, and turns back to me.

"Yeah. I'll help," he says, his voice like sandpaper. "Give me a day. I'll grease the wheels and get you a meeting. I can't promise anything will come of it, but I'll do what I can."

"Even after I told you we are mates, you'll still help me?"

"I want her to be happy. I don't care if it's me who brings her happiness, as long as she's actually happy."

"I hope you mean that, Voyt. I really, really do."

Because when this goes south, at least Evangeline will have someone who loves her that much.

I can do what I need to, knowing that.

4

EVAN

I have a strong urge to wear yoga pants and not get out of bed for a week. Or maybe I'll just eat enough ice cream to give myself a sugar coma and sleep for the next fifty years.

Yeah. That could work.

The funeral was last night, and I haven't left this room for approximately twenty-four hours. By my count, I have less than five minutes left before Aurelia either busts down the door or figures out how to jerry-rig an incendiary device and blow it off its hinges.

The new raw wood door the idiot twins installed is substantial enough, but nothing stops my bestie. Solid oak be damned.

I'm proved right not two minutes later when Asher ferries Aurelia and Mena into the room with him in a swath of black smoke, totally bypassing the door altogether.

Right. I should have thought of that.

"Are you getting subtle in your old age?" I croak from underneath my veritable cocoon of down blankets and pillows.

She doesn't answer me, she simply holds up a finger and covers her mouth with her other hand, swiftly but calmly walking to the bathroom. The retching that quickly bites at her heels tells me all I need to know.

"You think she'll figure it out on her own or should we tell her?" Mena asks me, but I have no freaking clue what she's talking about.

Whatever. I don't have the energy for this.

"Figure out what, Princess?" Asher inquires, but Mena doesn't answer him.

She just gives him a sweet look that from this angle tells me she thinks he's a silly, stupid man. He doesn't catch it, though, because he's too busy looking at her lips to notice anything else.

Barf.

"If I wanted to see the newbie lovers in action, I would have gone outside my room," I gripe, and for an extra barrier against love-sick assholes, I throw a pillow over my head.

Two smarmy doe-eyed lovers and one pukey best friend. If this is the cheer-up crew, I am so screwed.

A flush and the tap sounding from the open bathroom door is a relief. That is until I hear her brushing her teeth. With what has to be my toothbrush.

Umm. No, she did not. The gargle and spit that follows just pisses me off more.

"You're going to need a new toothbrush," Aurelia croaks from the doorway still looking green.

"Are you kidding me?" I screech from my fortress of pillows.

If she thinks this is getting me out of bed, she is sorely mistaken.

"Nope," she groans, shuffling over to the bed and shoving me over to lay down beside me.

She barely has her head on a stolen pillow when there is frantic banging on the new door.

"Aurelia?" Rhys frantically calls through the wood. "You okay, Gorgeous? Open this damn door!"

Mena stifles a snicker as she unlocks it for him, and he damn near bowls her over getting through the door to get to his wife. Before I can blink, he's on his knees next to her side of the bed, checking her forehead for fever.

I have no idea why. As far as I know, I have never heard of Phoenix getting sick. Ever. I look from them to Mena and Asher, who are cuddling in a single white leather slipper chair. I think I would rather be on the moon than see every single one of my friends right now. And it sucks.

I don't want to see people. I don't want to talk. I don't want to bear witness to a cute kiss or nuzzled hug. I want my Mom and Dad. I want to rip out the guts of whoever conspired to take them from me, and if I can't have that, then... I don't know what. I'm not sure I'll let myself want anything else.

Soon, the room is filled with my family. Ian, his face somber for probably the first time in his life, and then Aidan filing in behind him. Even Cam and Carver show up. Carver's superfluous eyepatch is jauntily flipped up showing a perfectly working eye. I think it is supposed to make me laugh, and in normal circumstances, it probably would.

And even though this room is filled with all the people I love, I feel more alone than ever. Their voices practically grate on my skin. They all want to know if I'm okay. They want to know what's next, why I sent West away. The questions aren't asked, but I know they're there. I feel them closing in on me.

But I don't have the answers. I don't know what's

next. I don't know if I'm okay. I'd venture a guess as to no—I'm not.

And West...

I sent him away because he would never choose me. I've been waiting for him to pick me—bind me—forever. He had all the time in the world, and he left me alone. And watching how quickly Mena and Asher succumbed to the bond. How little time it took... it just makes the century I've been waiting seem so much longer.

And Mama, Papa. My heart couldn't take much more. I needed to cut the dead weight, so he had to go.

"Hey," Aurelia whispers, pulling me out of the stirrings of a top-notch panic attack. "Want to go beat the shit out of something? I'll even hold the heavy bag for you," she offers, her voice soft in the newly loud room.

It is a kindness she's offering me, a reason to leave without a fuss, and I appreciate it more than I can say.

"Get dressed. I'll kick these assholes out," she assures me, and I feel my lips pull into a pathetic attempt at a smile.

I think I'm at a point in my life where I don't want to have to be grateful, but I am.

Aurelia ushers everyone from my room, allowing me a few moments to collect myself before I go kick the crap out of a heavy bag. But I don't dawdle. Instead, I move as quickly as I can through the motions of opening a brand new toothbrush and attacking my teeth with it, throwing on some clothes and heading out the door to the gym. At this point, I don't even know if my socks match, but I don't really give a crap.

I have the single-minded focus of a woman who is systematically avoiding her problems. No thinking, just doing.

Instead of walking, I travel to the gym located on the top floor of the cliff house and watch Aurelia string up the hundred-and-fifty-pound heavy bag on a wall-mounted L-bracket like she's tying her freaking shoelaces. After she hooks the bag, she doesn't look at me expectantly, she just moves on, wrapping her hands, waiting for me to be ready.

The space is mostly open, the weights and lifting platforms closer to the edges, and the center left open for sparring. I love this room, and if it weren't for the three full walls of floor to ceiling windows, I would have claimed it for myself.

Papa said it wasn't safe for me—it had too many points of entry. It couldn't be fortified. My suite on the second floor doesn't have any windows. As an interior room, I'm boxed in. I hate it. I see these windows, and I realize how naive and sheltered I've been. Skipping along happy when others were keeping me safe.

It's San Francisco all over again—me thinking I know better when everyone else had to watch my back, had to worry for me. I should know better.

"You about done wallowing?" she asks bracing herself behind the bag, and her dumb question is like a red flag in front of a bull.

"Wallowing? Really? You want to know if I'm done wallowing?" I roar, throwing a solid haymaker into the bag—my hands still unwrapped.

I don't move her an inch, and it just pisses me off. The stain of the blood on the canvas makes it worse.

"Pfft. Weak sauce. You've done better in your sleep," she needles me with a sneering little smile on her face.

The feral scream ripping up my throat surprises me, but not Aurelia. She looks bored, unruffled. My next punch doesn't hit the bag—it doesn't hit anything at all. I clutch at nothing but air as Aurelia moves blindingly fast avoiding my fists at every turn. I can't make myself stop the advance on her, and with every single failed hit, my anger grows.

The phase comes against my will, my fangs ripping through my lips, my talons erupting from my fingertips. I can't stop. I try to rush her, herd her into the corner, but I can't seem to close in on her the way I want to. She's always one step ahead, and with every failed strike, the single-minded pain in my chest chips away.

But in its place, the anger grows—the fury and regret and wrath.

I know what to do now. I know how I'm going to fix this mess. And with my last punch, I stop mere millimeters in front of her nose, pulling back just enough so Aurelia knows I could have hit her square in the face if I wanted to.

"Feel better?" she asks, and I realize she meant for me to lose it. She wanted me to vent this noxious poison brewing in my gut.

"A bit, but more importantly, I know what to do now," I say, my breaths coming out ragged.

She nods at me and strolls over to a tucked away mini-fridge filled with water and tosses me a bottle. I chug it down in three large swallows.

"I think Voyt had a good idea. I think if I gain support from the lower echelon of the Wraith community, I can face the head families with more than just my father's word at my back. Vengeance can't be the only goal here. If it is, then I will have nothing left when this is all over."

And I won't give those bastards the satisfaction of beating me after I burn them to the ground.

5

WEST

The Emerson's house makes me uncomfortable, like having an arm lopped off in shark-infested waters uncomfortable. It isn't just that the house—no, this structure could only be described as a mansion—is bigger than any home John and Olivia ever owned. What looks to be three stories with an additional stone-faced basement level tucked into a man-made hill, the only word I can use to describe it is vast.

And white. White paint, white stone, white columns.

The ground level is ensconced in a true southern-style wrap around porch with open slotted railings, complete with ceiling fans and chaise loungers. The second story has more of the same, only with an open-air balcony. The abundance of white is intermittently broken up by tall cobalt planters spilling riots of flowers down their sides. It's like a home and garden show vomited all over this place.

It isn't the lawn trimmed within an inch of its life, or that there isn't a single out of place leaf, twig, or weed to be found on the sprawling expanse of turf butting up against a forest so dense the waning sunlight refuses to filter through the leaves.

No.

The source of the pit in my stomach is the level of security and personnel surrounding the sprawling expanse of land butting the shore of Heritage Lake. Men lounging on chaises appear to be enjoying the sunset, but I know for certain they're covert security by their body language. None of the men are relaxed in their posture. Backs straight as an arrow, their heads move on a continuous scan of their sections, ready and waiting for a threat. Add that to the boats in the lake that only seem to pass to and fro in front of the property and nowhere else.

But these men don't see me yet—at least I don't think they do.

I traveled into the dense forest cradling the estate a football field away from the property line so I could assess the property without an audience. Too bad I'm one hundred percent sure I'm being watched. Either by cameras or people, I can't tell yet, but a finger of apprehension rakes its sharp claw down my back, and I know for certain I have eyes on me.

I suppose it's possible there's someone else out here, but I don't think so.

I've been on this earth for over six hundred years, and I haven't lived this long without learning a few things.

One of those things is how to spot surveillance.

I notice at least three black bullet cameras hidden strategically in the branches of a few southern red oak trees. That should be enough this far from the house, but the most worrisome—and definitely the most dangerous—are the five proximity sensors embedded into the bark of the Virginia pine and white birch trees to my left and right.

Proximity sensors that at this very moment are blinking red.

Okay. Stay calm. You were invited here. Invited... right.

I put my hands in the pockets of my jeans, cease my subversive study of their equipment, and start walking on my booted feet toward the house. Manners dictate that popping into someone's living room is considered bad form, so I mosey on, strolling as if I'm supposed to be here. Technically, I am.

As soon as Voyt told Walter Emerson—the patriarch of the Emerson family—that I had been released from my charge as Evangeline's Guardian, he wasted no time inviting me to his home for a meeting. I believe the word Voyt used was '*clamored.*'

While I'm not sure why old Walter thought it would be the best plan to have Voyt be the go-between, who am I to argue with a man nearly twice my age?

Feeling the thinning of the dense, humid air in front of me heralding the traveling of a Wraith, I have never been happier I don't have a single weapon on me as I am at this moment. If I came here armed I have no idea what would happen.

I don't know my place here with these people. By the looks of this house, they are going to take one look at the exposed ink on my arms, my gauges, my long hair, and they're going to make up their minds.

With John, at least I knew he gave a shit. With these people? Who knows.

Raising my hands in surrender, I try to appear as non-threatening as I can manage—which is difficult for someone six and a half feet tall—and wait. Before I can blink, five Wraiths travel into the space in front of me, all drawing down on my head. They look nothing like the guards on the decks and on the lawn of the house. These men are dressed in head-to-toe black suits, have a *'don't fuck with me, or I'll end you'* look to their faces, and an overt demeanor that screams Guardian.

Even their hair is the same. The lot of them have close-cropped, almost buzz-cuts. The only thing differentiating them is the color of their hair.

Well, hello to you too.

The men don't move—hell, they don't even blink— and we stand in this putridly tense silence waiting for each other to make a move. It might as well be me.

"If this is how you welcome invited guests, you all need some serious hospitality training," I droll, calm on the outside while I curse myself for not bringing at least one blade with me.

"West Carmichael?" the one in the front asks.

He might be the leader, but then again, he might not. He is barely distinguishable from the rest, and the level of uniformity makes me very uneasy.

As if I wasn't already coming out of my skin.

"Yep, that's me. I have a meeting with Walter Emerson in five minutes. May I ask you lower your weapons? Scooter there on the end is looking a little twitchy."

And he is. The poor, young Guardian at the back left looks barely a century old—if that—and it shows. It isn't that he's smaller than the rest—he's not, he's just as tall and broad as his brethren—it is more he seems to be the only uneasy one.

Someone has heard of me.

But when I look into his eyes, it isn't the spark of recognition I expect.

No.

This young one has seen things. Terrible things. And I don't know what he's witnessed, but I remember that look. It is one I used to see in the mirror every day before I got away from the people who made me. Before I changed my name. Before John got me out of the gutter.

Masking my reaction, I still feel my teeth clench. I'm an idiot for not bringing weapons.

The leader nods and all five firearms lower at once. He about-faces turning his back to me like a damn robot and marches toward the house, the other four men following suit.

"Follow us," he orders over his shoulder, and I have never wanted to do something less in my whole life than I want to walk into whatever is in that pretty house.

But I will. For my Angel.

The trek seems to take ages, even at the fast clip of the Guardians that appear to have a serious sticks up their asses. When we finally reach the sprawling porch,

I'm told to wait. The house is even more perfect up close. No filth from pollen or weather mars the pristine white-planked porch. The chaises are perfectly fluffed, not a pillow or cushion out of place. The flowering pots are deadheaded—not a single wilted flower to be found.

This place creeps me the hell out.

"Someone will be right with you," the leader says, breaking me from my inspection, and four of the five travel from the porch as one. The fifth—the youngest— catches my eye and gives a slight shake of his head before traveling himself.

My gut clenches, the pit in my stomach growing larger. I want to get out of here. I want to travel from this picture perfect hell and go back to my Angel.

But I can't. I can't leave without making sure she stays alive. Rock, meet hard place.

Before I can change my mind and get the fuck out of here, the ornate front door opens. The tall, blonde woman behind it, looks to be no more than twenty-five human years old. But with our kind, she could be anywhere from twenty-five to twelve hundred and nine for all I know. The hardened cast to her honey-brown eyes tells me she's either very old or has lived through Hell.

My guess is the latter.

She's dressed to match the house. Prim, proper, and

white—white dress, white shoes, white pearls. What is with these people and the white? Her makeup is tasteful but subdued, and her hair is pulled back into a bun at the nape of her neck like Evangeline does when she wants to look classy.

I hate it when my Angel pulls her riot of curls back.

Focus, dipshit.

"Mr. Carmichael?" she asks as if she isn't sure.

I'm a big man and the ink puts people off, but this lady looks like she's ready to bolt. Based on the pit in my gut, the young Guardian's response and this woman's face, I'm thinking this is probably the worst fucking idea I've ever had.

But intuition tells me this is the family. This is the place. These are the people behind so much unneeded death. And as much as I want to leave, as much as I want to travel from this place and never darken their door again, Evangeline comes first. I tip my chin up in the affirmative and wait for her to either open the door or tell me to go to hell.

"Please, come in," she says as she opens the door wider for me to enter displaying more and more of the opulence.

But I don't really see it. What I do see is the way her eyes flit down to the floor. The way her shoulders turn inward like a wounded little bird.

She's either seriously afraid of me, or she's been abused.

I'm getting real tired of this shit. Who hurts women? Aurelia. Mena. Two females that didn't deserve the hell they've lived with. Now this poor girl. What kind of sick bastard does this?

As I take a step to pass her, she whispers. The word doesn't register at first, but when the same five Guardians travel into the room accompanied by several more men, what she said makes sense.

She was trying to save me. Just like that young Guardian tried to warn me.

She was telling me to *run*.

6

EVAN

"You want to do what now?"

I studied the plum polish on my fingernails, in an attempt not to maim one of my oldest confidants. There was no *want* about it. I was going to do this whether Aidan and Cam liked it or not.

Once I was confident I wouldn't launch myself across the room to punch Cam in the face, I lifted my gaze.

"What is so difficult to understand? Papa did not address the concerns of our people for almost a year, Cam. Support for the Black family is likely in the toilet, half of our species has been slaughtered, and the ones that weren't already in hiding, are wishing they'd found a good rock to retire under. If I want to actually be a Queen, it's high time I started acting like one."

Cam sputters, huffs, and then mashes his lips together in indignation. I'm right, and he knows it.

"I'm not talking about gracing the high and mighty with my presence. I'm talking about the regular folk, the people who are just trying to live their lives without a target on their backs. I'm talking about organized, methodical ways of obtaining souls, keeping Wraiths fed and healthy before they lose their minds."

Uncrossing my legs, I lean forward on the couch, pinning Cam with the truth.

"I need support, Cam, and I'm not going to get it from those stuffy bastards who sit up on high no matter what the Council says. If I'm going to be their Queen, I need to earn it."

Cam shoves to his feet and starts pacing the length of the living room, pausing at every revolution to eye the liquor cabinet like he would love a bourbon.

"I really hate it when you're right," he grumbles. "But right or not, how in the Fates are we supposed to keep you safe?"

"We can bring a team of security," Aidan offers from his formerly silent section of the couch.

Yeah, that would go over well. *Hi! I'm your Queen, but obviously, I can't defend myself so here's a bunch of huge men. You don't mind if they come in your house too, right?*

"Absolutely not. Just you two. This is a peacekeeping goodwill mission, not an invasion."

Cam's face goes beet red, and I can see him grinding his teeth from here.

"I don't know why you two are pissing and moaning. At least your charge doesn't have to go back into a society that has practiced mass genocide on their own people," Asher pipes up from the door to the office.

He's spent the last twenty-four hours trying to talk Mena and Aurelia out of their current plan to help restructure the power vacuum left with Iva's death and Nicola's absence. He isn't having any more luck than my Guardians.

Mena hugs her husband from behind, resting her chin on his shoulder. "We're doing this. You're just going to have to get over it."

Nodding, I speared Cam and Aidan with a hard look.

"We're doing this," I insist.

I just hope it doesn't come to bite me in the ass.

AURELIA, RHYS, MENA, AND ASHER LEFT THE CLIFF HOUSE THE same time I left to go on my pilgrimage to meet Wraiths that were anything but the filth of the head families. They needed to get back to their people, and with Nicola missing, who knew what kind of chaos they were walking into. I wasn't a huge fan of the division—and I'm still not—but letting your people hang in the wind is the reason both our factions were imploding.

The first family on my list were the Webers. A modest family with a small homestead in the foothills of the Canadian Rockies. We traveled to the edge of their property, ambling up the driveway at a sedate pace.

I wanted to give them plenty of time to prepare themselves for my visit, just not as much time as a phone call would provide.

This far away from a large populace, I wonder how they stay fed. It wasn't like people died out here in the country every day or even every week. I pause my pondering when a large man exits the home, waiting for us on the porch. Mocha-skinned and roughly a billion feet tall—okay, probably close to seven, but still—he waits patiently for us to traverse the driveway, parking himself in one of the several wooden rocking chairs peppered on the covered porch.

The three of us stop at the steps leading up to the

house, waiting for the man to acknowledge us. After about thirty seconds, I had enough with the waiting bit.

"Mr. Weber?" I call. "Are you Xavier Weber, sir?"

He nods, still rocking, looking off into the distance.

"You that new Queen everyone's going on about?"

I worry about the level of talk and what they're probably saying, but I don't tell him that.

"I am. Would you be willing to speak to me?"

The man stops his rocking and turns to eye me up and down. Not in a rude way but in an assessing one.

"I suppose that would be alright. Your guard dogs can even come in too, but they'll leave their weapons outside. I don't allow weapons of any kind in my home."

"Absolutely fucking not," Cam growls under his breath, stepping in front of me, putting himself in between this behemoth of a man.

But his words weren't said quietly enough so Xavier doesn't hear him, and it's all I can do not to punch him in his fool face. Tapping Cam on the shoulder, I wait for him to turn his head.

"Your asshole, uber-protective ways are only hurting my chances of looking like a competent leader," I hiss between gritted teeth. "Knock it the fuck off, or I'm going to have to behead your ass right here."

Cam's eyes widen a fraction before he steps aside, allowing me to address Xavier once again.

"I apologize for any insult. Cameron has been with my family since before I was born. He has trouble letting me participate in things he deems as a detriment to my safety. There have been a few threats to my life in these last few days, so my Guardians are a little twitchy. Are you or your family a detriment to my safety, Mr. Weber?"

"No, your highness."

"Do you mind if we talk on your porch? That way you and I can talk freely, and my Guardians aren't overly concerned with my safety. How'd that be?"

"That would be just fine."

It takes less than five minutes to realize that Xavier Weber is a friendly mountain of a man. Of Dominican and German ancestry, he and his family relocated to this property to avoid being exterminated by Iva. But they miss their home and the ease of obtaining food. They miss the warm weather.

And they want to know if it's safe to return.

"A good politician would tell you what you want to hear, but I've never been a politician, and I don't plan to be. The truth is, I don't know. Iva is ashes, but I'm not sure if that's permanent. The newest Phoenix leader is mated to a Wraith, so relations between our species should smooth out, but I can't promise no one will act like a jackass and ruin it. My goal is to get you home, to make sure you're fed, and to keep you and your family safe."

Xavier gave me another one of his assessing looks. "I like your plan, highness, but you know I'm not the man you need to convince."

I'd known that tidbit, but I'd hoped it wasn't true. My sources told me that Xavier was one of the most respected Wraiths in the community. The problem was, his veneration was second to a man that pretty much hated my father.

"The man you need to convince is Trenton Price."

Figures.

EVAN—1928—LOS ANGELES, CA

The first time I met West Carmichael, I was singing at a speakeasy in Los Angeles. My parents didn't know where I was, and for the first time in a long time, neither did Aurelia. Hiding from a Seer is probably the hardest thing I've ever done, but a special cloaking amulet from a witch friend worked wonders.

It was pretty. A sapphire the size of my thumbnail set in a silver filigree setting hanging from a thin chain that rests just below my collarbone. It wasn't the nicest piece of jewelry I owned, but it was my favorite.

Maybe because it granted me my freedom.

Or maybe because it matched my royal blue silk charmeuse gown to perfection. I used to hate dressing up, but this lone frock made me feel like a woman. It was an off the shoulder number with a daring sweetheart neckline—far ahead of its time. It fit like a second skin until it hit my thighs then flared out like a calla lily into a delicate but short train. It may not have been the most comfortable dress I owned, but it made me feel like a sexy siren. Something that with my diminutive height, I rarely felt.

I was alone—finally alone even in this sea of people– after so much time with the ones I loved breathing down my neck. It was like a vacation. I needed something of my own. A secret, a life, something to break away from my family. Something that didn't say princess or royalty.

Something that let me just be me. Singing was it for me.

I was ending my five-song set with a favorite of mine, an old Jane Greene song when I saw him. I'd glimpsed him around town a few times, when I was shopping by myself or when I watched a boxing match at the Olympic Auditorium, a scandalous activity for an unchaperoned young lady.

But we'd never met.

He was handsome, I even daresay beautiful. If you

can call a man like that beautiful. Tall—taller than anyone in the room by nearly a whole head—and built so powerfully he made the other men look like pitiful adolescents dressed up in their daddy's clothes. It was difficult to tell if his hair was as dark as it seemed in the low light of the secret club, but it appeared so in the dim.

Dressed to the nines in a brilliant black suit, he moved with grace through the crowd until he found his seat at the only open table in the joint, folding his huge frame into the chair with the grace of a jaguar.

Papa had taken me to Brazil when I was just a little girl, and we saw the big cats roam the rainforests. He moved just like one of those jungle cats, scanning the room for prey and threats, watching everything with casual disinterest, as if he could take or leave the sights and sounds and people. As if he were bored in this raucous party that seemed to never end.

But when his eyes hit mine... I was struck dumb, and I nearly flubbed the last three words of the chorus. His eyes were green, the color somewhere between jade and emerald, and framed in lashes so thick it was a wonder his eyelids could carry the weight of them.

I could tell he was like me—a Wraith—but despite his rather comely appearance, I wanted nothing to do with him. Better he think I was just some boozy siren losing her morals in the backroom of some secret gin joint than to know what I really was.

A prim and proper princess hiding out as if I wasn't of age, as if I was a young one. As if I wasn't more than a child. And maybe... maybe, compared to the rest of them, I might be.

Hell, I was only in my forties. To everyone else, I was practically a baby.

But I didn't feel like a baby. I didn't feel like I was some wayward child, but after San Francisco... it would be a long time before anyone trusted me with anything ever again.

On that troubled thought, I finished my song, made my way to the coat room, snatched my deep pile cranberry red velvet coat from its hanger despite the ire of the rather irritated coat check clerk and made my way through a group of slightly handsy revelers out the back entrance of the club.

This particular door led to a deserted alleyway, but I paid it no mind. I wasn't afraid. Sure, I was a woman alone at night, but I only needed to get out of sight of potential on-lookers before traveling back home.

But I didn't see them until they were within touching distance, and for this lot, was more than too close.

They were three steps past drunk and five steps past

evil. I could smell it. Both the musty perfume of cheap alcohol and the mouthwatering scent of a filthy soul. I felt my fangs lengthen behind my lips as their souls called to me, and I fought not to phase on the spot.

Their clothes were in disarray, shirts half untucked, shoes scuffed, hair rumpled, and taking them in, I felt a little fear as my hunger grew.

I'd heard stories. Whispers of what could happen to women out alone. But I wasn't some weak human woman, and I wasn't helpless. I may abhor killing humans, but if it came down to them or me, I'd pick me ten times out of ten.

At their leers and snide little jeers, I felt my talons start to grow—my phase roiling under my skin, spoiling for a fight when I wanted anything but one.

But they never laid a finger on me.

Like an avenging angel, a large shadow loomed over my shoulder, blocking the light of the electric street lamp just thirty feet away at the mouth of the alley.

The men didn't have time to run. Or scream. Or fight. They were dead before they took their next breath. And standing before me was the Wraith from before. His hair was slightly mussed, but not one other thing was out of place.

I'd known I'd seen him before. But the way he'd intervened... The way he'd stood, breaths heaving, shoulders set, jaw clenched, eyeing me with censure and disdain, I knew. I'd thought since I'd been home so much, they would forgo assigning me a Guardian. A babysitter.

After twenty-two years, I thought I had slipped my leash. I was wrong.

I wanted to cry, but that was a luxury I wouldn't allow myself. Not in front of this beautiful man who seemed to despise me so much.

"Guardian?" I asked, my voice clogged with the tears I held onto by the skin of my teeth, but I already knew the answer.

Averting my eyes, I refused to watch his face shame me more. But because I was looking at my sapphire silk shoes, I missed his eyes dilating. I missed his breath go from labored to non-existent.

I missed seeing him realize I was his mate.

"Are you going to tell my father?" I asked, still looking at my shoes, but I never got an answer.

When I looked up again, the large Wraith and the three men were gone.

And I'd never even got his name.

EVAN

West has been on my mind more not less since I released him. Maybe I just need something to obsess about instead of thinking about my parents. Really? Who wouldn't? But the more I ponder it, the more I think maybe I just miss him.

After the first day he intervened outside that speakeasy, West has been a fixture in my life. My own personal hulking shadow saving me from myself. I want him—more than I'm willing to admit out loud—and it just pisses me off. I snap my eyes open as my feet touch the pavement.

This is how the bulk of our people live? Here? In Mayberry?

I think this as I walk up the brick-paved drive of a pretty, middle-class house, in a middle-class neighborhood, in a nice, quiet, small town. This is the seventh family I've called on, and it shocks me every time. This house is no different than the others I've visited—a different style of decorating and cars, maybe—but the theme is the same.

These are normal people. Normal folk who live regular lives in ordinary neighborhoods. Just living their lives. Two point five kids and a labradoodle, having brunch on Sundays, fucking normal. Not rich, not having more money than they can use in ten lifetimes, not evil or hungry for power. Real people with jobs and lives, on the PTA and neighborhood watch.

They just also happen to eat the souls of the damned on the weekends.

Here I thought all Wraiths—my own people—were greedy, scheming, shitty individuals, but the families I've met over the last week are decidedly not. They are friendly and hospitable and humble.

I have never felt at ease with a single member of the head families. Fearing the use of the wrong fork at dinner or tripping over my own feet—which happens more than one would think. I have never wanted to get to know them or speak casually with them or even give them the time of day. Too many chances to fuck up in front of them and have whispers about some random slip-up filter back to my parents. Not that they would mind. But these people... these are the people I would protect. And if these are the people Voyt has been helping, my respect for him has shot up by about three hundred percent.

I've avoided this house and this man for as long as I could.

My heels click on the pale gray brick paver pathway leading to the front porch of an elegant-but-simple craftsman-style home in the small town of Warrenton,

Virginia. Cam and Aidan are at my back, looking less menacing than they have been over the last week. After each dismissal, each refusal, I knew exactly where I needed to go.

But this family, this house, was the one I was dreading. Their support—or dissention—would determine which way the domino would fall.

The Price clan was not among my father's biggest supporters. In fact, I'm fairly certain Trenton Price didn't even like my father. While they might not have been friends, Papa respected him. I remember them having heated debates about the problems in our society. Usually, it would end up in a sparring match, but Trenton and my father would end up coming to an agreement about whatever had them stirred up after they tried to kick each other's asses.

Things were going fine—or at least semi-amiable—up until about a year ago. I think this was when Mama was starting to get sick. Trenton and Papa's usually good-natured arguments went from fine to not fine pretty quickly.

Before I can take the first step up the porch stairs, Trenton whips open the door. He isn't a small man, well over six feet and solidly built. Sable brown hair clipped tight around his ears and long on top, clear blue eyes and a rocking beard.

I always thought Trenton was a level-headed man. I admired him. Usually the issues he brought to my father, I agreed with. Maybe not his proposed execution of them, but still.

Right now, though, I'm not certain old Trent has all his marbles. Especially since he has a double barreled shotgun aimed right at my chest.

7

WEST

WELL, THIS IS A FINE MESS I'VE PUT MYSELF IN.

The trek to my current accommodations was long and arduous. Through the bottom floor of the pristine, white house, down two flights of stairs—one of them so old and rickety I was sure they would break under the weight of my left boot—and along a lengthy stone hallway passing cell after cell, to my new abode. All the while, I have to fight my natural instincts to not maim, murder, and kill because I had the barrel of a gun jammed against the back of my head, and the shithead holding the weapon wasn't nice about it either.

This isn't the first time I've been held at gunpoint, nor is it the first time I've been held captive. My life up to this point hasn't been sunshine and roses, but for the years I was Evangeline's Guardian, it was pretty close. I was a part of something. I had a family—better than the one I was born into.

I should have known I wouldn't get to keep it. I should have known it would all go to hell some time. *And that some time is right about now.*

My new home is a small, ten-by-six stone cell with a stainless steel cot bolted to the right wall and matching toilet on the left. The stone appears ancient, and I would venture a guess I'm in some not-so-forgotten cellar or dungeon, or possibly, given the location and style of the house, the long-abandoned slave quarters. Just thinking that gives me the willies.

The burgundy-black of long dried bloodstains on the floor and walls does nothing to help matters, either.

I suppose the man-made hill the house sits on makes much more sense now, but the water table must have risen since the structure was initially dug because the walls and floor are practically weeping with moisture. The smell of mold, mildew, and the stench of torture and pain are all rank within the dungeon.

All I've had for the last hour is the bare metal cot, the toilet of doom, the wet stone walls, and the solid steel door that could substitute for a bank vault.

Oh, and silence. I've had a fair bit of that.

The first thing I tried as soon as they slammed my cell's door was traveling, but I got nothing and nowhere —just a black mist ping-ponging against the walls. I'm guessing some witchy juju is at play here.

Fabulous.

I want to pace, but I can't make it more than two strides before hitting a wall. I want to punch through the stone, but I have a feeling I'm going to have to avoid injury as much as possible. I have a feeling some serious pain is coming my way.

I have a feeling I've been betrayed.

I cannot believe I trusted that fucker. My gut lied to me. It told me I could trust him. It said he was the in for me here. If I ever see Voyt Garrison again, I'm going to rip his fucking head off.

When the cell door groans open, I tense like a coiled snake, ready to blow through whoever stands between me and freedom. I'm not thinking of what's beyond the door. I'm not thinking of anything but not dying in this little slice of hell. So when Voyt's head comes into view, I feel the beginnings of a sadistic smile stretch across my face before I can stop it.

Just the man I wanted to see, I think as I strike. Lunging across the last few steps to grab him by his perfectly ironed shirtfront, slamming him into the closest wall. I take the extreme pleasure in watching his head bounce off the rough stone. He's only stunned for a second before the phase comes over him, and even though he tries to speak, I wrench him back and slam him again. He's ready for it this time, and the strike to my forearms is hard enough that I nearly lose my grip on him.

Nearly, but not quite. Then, I start hitting him in every soft-tissue spot I can reach. Abdomen, kidneys, solar plexus, are all hammered by my fists before he breaks my hold. He doesn't attack while I recover, only throws his hands up to block my next blow. If I weren't so enraged, I would have picked up on it. I would have noticed he never attacked me back, only blocked me, punch for punch, strike for strike.

I don't notice this until it is almost too late. Then, my brain catches up with my body, and I stifle the blow I was aiming to his throat. One more inch, and he would be dead.

"Is there a reason you're neglecting to fight back, Voyt? Because unless you give me a good reason, I'm ripping your fucking throat out," I growl through my fangs.

"Yes, and if you could manage to calm down, I'll tell you," he says with a sardonic yet relieved expression on his face.

He gets a reluctant nod from me, but he barely pauses to wait for my response.

"I have too much to get out and limited amount of time to do it. I didn't betray you. I swear. As far as I know, Walter is not going to keep you here. He is going to interrogate you, though, and this is what I'm twitchy about. I think he has other people down here. He has some freaky shit going on in this house, and Claire looks like a damn POW," he whispers furiously as he rips his hands through his hair.

"Who is Claire?"

"Claire Emerson. The woman who answered the door? She's Walter's daughter," he informs me.

This bit of info is shocking. She tried to warn me. If she's Walter's daughter, why would she stick her neck out like that? Who knows what is really going on here. Without a good reason, I trust this Claire. She tried to help me, I think, and I even though I can't decide if it is a ruse, I trust those wounded-looking shoulders before I'd trust a smile. Those shoulders said victim, they said pain. Those shoulders told the truth.

"She told me to run, and one of his Guardians signaled for me to leave. I don't think you know what's going on here anymore than I do," I tell him, regretful I asked him to help me.

"Probably not. I'm flying blind here, man. I had no

idea... I'm used to petty stuff, West, not this duplicitous horse shit. I have no idea what I'm supposed to do," he admits, and I feel bad for the guy, I do, but not enough to let him off the hook.

I need him to do one thing for me, and I need him to keep his head.

"Just keep calm. I think I can talk my way out of this. Maybe. But if you get out of here, and I don't, you tell Evangeline everything, okay? You tell her I was right. She'll know what you mean," I instruct him, my tone pleading.

I know what I'm telling him to do, and I don't want her in danger, but she needs to know. She needs to know I didn't forget about her. I didn't abandon her. She needs to know who she can trust.

Voyt takes a deep breath, squares his shoulders and gets his shit together. He gives me a nod and turns to leave before I say the absolute last thing I ever wanted to say.

"Keep her safe, Voyt. Promise," I order, my voice like it's been run over broken glass. I think it is the rawness of my voice that stops him in his tracks.

He never turns back around, but as he pushes that cell door wider to leave, he whispers, "I will."

I'll hold him to that.

In this life or the next.

8

EVAN

Trent has lost his mind, I think as I raise my hands in surrender. The three of us have stopped in our tracks on the immaculate brick paver pathway, waiting for the crazy man to decide if he's going to kill us or not.

I hope not, but with the way my life is going right now, I'm not holding out hope for some miracle.

"Get off my land, Evangeline. Whatever you want, I'm not helping you," Trent growls, stepping across the threshold onto the porch, and I see my opening.

I don't wait for Aidan or Cam who I can tell are still trying to come up with an exit strategy. I love them like brothers, but they will just mess this up for me.

I don't wait for Trent to say another word, either.

Who knows what has that man in a twist. Instead of the showdown he probably expects, I travel just to the side of the open door and wrench the gun right out of his hands, tossing it to Cam with one hand and with the other, I grab the top cartilage of his ear and bend his big ass frame to my lips.

"That is no way to treat your Queen. Apologize. Now," I hiss into his ear. When his mouth screws up into a grimace but no apology passes his lips, I decide he needs a lesson. Before he knows what hit him, his nose is bleeding, and he's flat on his back on his own porch with my boot digging into his chest.

"You were saying?" I ask on a growl. I haven't phased, and I don't need to. I can do plenty all on my girly lonesome, *thank you very much.*

The crazed smile that breaks across his face is mildly disturbing and a bit endearing. He looks like a proud papa and his favorite child just learned to walk, or at least in my case, learned how to kick someone's ass.

"Evangeline, my Queen, how nice to see you again. Welcome to my home. Please do come in," he says genially enough that I remove my boot heel from his ribs.

"Trent, good to see you. I have a favor to ask. You up for it?" I ask as I smile sweetly down to him.

His smile is manic, but I pay it no mind. Trent is Mercury personified.

"Absolutely."

My plan—at least to me—seems like common sense, but to the head families, it will be seen as an act of aggression if not an all-out call for war. I don't want much; I just want them to use the manners they failed to learn in kindergarten. Hell, kindergarten wasn't even invented when these people were getting their feet in this world. Maybe their parents neglected to teach them the basics.

I'm sitting on a dainty chaise in a sitting room better suited for a *Gone with the Wind* reenactment rather than the super duper important head family meeting I'm supposed to be leading.

I'd wanted it to be in a conference room.

I'd wanted to pay each of the families a visit.

But Aurelia gave me some impeccable—albeit unwanted—advice.

"You have to make sure they underestimate you. Surprise is your friend here," she'd said, and she's right.

It doesn't matter if I dress the part in a power business suit with my hair pulled back or if I'm in a petticoat and corset, these stodgy old farts aren't going to give me the time of day anyway.

I'll have to make them.

By force if necessary.

The said stodgy bastards are all in attendance, thankfully, and I don't have to send someone to reel them in. Carver wanted that job, and I don't blame him. Twenty years of deceit makes a lot of bitter in one's stomach. I'd want to hunt the bastards down too. Alas, each of the head families has a representative here to listen to me even if they'd rather eat dog shit than hear me talk.

Vincent Stein, a lithe, if aged, gentleman sits to my left, casually reclined in a great leather wingback, his left ankle is coolly resting on his right knee, and he's sipping my father's scotch. He doesn't appear old per se, but rather he looks like a thirty-five-year-old man has gone gray very early in his life. He's likely edging on over a thousand if I could take a guess, and unlike my father, he will probably be around for a few more centuries.

I can feel my lips start to curl at that thought but rein in my ire. I can't start off this way.

To Vincent's right is Walter Emerson, and good-looking guy or not, he gives me bad vibes in a pretty major way. It isn't just that his sons, Devereux and

Sampson died trying to save me. Anyone would feel awful for that, but I don't feel awful, exactly, more I feel indifferent.

Devereux could have gotten us out of San Francisco. He could have gone back to my father instead of traipsing us all over the country. He was considerably older than I was, and at twenty-one, I had neither the necessary skills to fight myself nor the understanding of security as I do now. I may have caused the destruction in the aftermath, and I will hate myself until the day I die for taking so many lives, but I did not take theirs. Devereux and Sam died because they were too scared to go back to Papa with men on their heels. It may have taken me nearly a century to get over it, but I don't feel the guilt of their loss like I used to.

Walter's eyes are dead—not like he's masking his emotions—like he doesn't have any in the first place. His face is animated enough, but those eyes... pale gray irises thickly lined with long, black lashes which are at odds with his platinum blonde hair have to be the creepiest things in the known universe. He's handsome—taller than average height, square jaw, trim waist, decent upper body. He's not West by any stretch of the imagination, but he's built solidly enough.

I do not need to be thinking of West right now.

Halting my inspection of Walter, I move to the rest

of the men in the room. Each of them handsome in their own right, but they all lack a significant emotional trait that is crucial. They do not give one single ripe shit about anyone or anything but themselves.

And because of that, I will have to be a hypocrite.

Staying in the same lounged position, on my completely unnecessary but decorative piece of furniture with Aidan and Cam at my back, I address the room.

"Wraiths are the most hated faction of the Ethereal. Do you know why they hate us? Because they fear us," I announce, and my saying this pulls a smile or positive gesture from every man in this room except for the men I trust.

This tells me all I need to know.

"Ruling by fear is why we are dwindling into nothing. Other factions won't help us. Witches think we are no better than Demons. The Phoenixes—except for a slight few—have practically stomped us into extinction. Warlocks and Shapeshifters think we are no better than cockroaches because a few have tainted the reputation of us all. Stealing from other factions. Threatening Hell to any that oppose them. Extortion of services and money to avoid getting sent downstairs. Trafficking Witches and Warlocks to the highest bidder for Fates only know what. Murder. Sedition. Mutiny," I accuse, my eyes landing on Walter at the last word. "All these crimes have been committed by a person in this room, their family, someone under their care, an employee— doesn't matter. As of this moment, it will stop. My father may have turned a blind eye, but I won't. We have an alliance with the Phoenixes now. Their newest leader, Mena Constantine, is mated with a Wraith. The Primary is Aurelia Constantine, my closest friend and the woman who took down Iva. As far as I'm concerned, all grievances with the Phoenixes have been squashed. Now, it is up to you to help me in this endeavor."

"And what would you have us do?" Vincent asks, and I can tell by his tone, he actually gives a shit.

He is really asking me because he wants to know. My relief in this is extinguished when Walter cuts in.

"It doesn't matter what she would have us do. This little girl isn't a Queen. She's barely over a century of unmated pussy," he says with a sneer, and he gets a butter wouldn't melt in my mouth smile in return.

My bland smile must prove something to him because he sits back in his chair and sips from his tumbler of my father's fucking scotch.

He doesn't get a swallow in before I've traveled to him and smashed that glass against his misogynistic face. While he's still stunned, I wrench him from his seat and bounce his head off an end table and then use his hair as a handle and drag him like a broken puppet to his feet. He can't keep them, and I feel the hair start ripping from his scalp as I speak.

"Using fear as a deterrent does not work for most people. Fear breeds unrest, unrest breeds hate, hate breeds war. You, gentlemen, have fucked around and done nothing for so long, we're at the late stage. I want you to stop whatever scams you have going on. Whatever nefarious activities your family, friends, employees, your second cousins twice removed has in the fire. Doesn't matter. Whatever it is, it stops now. You will investigate and eliminate these operations. Eliminate but not kill. You will bring them to me, and I will deal with them. We will be doing things very differently from now on, gentlemen," I inform them, still holding up Walter by his hair.

"Is this you not leading by fear?" Vincent asks, and by his smile, I can tell he's proud.

"I said fear doesn't work for most people. For some, it is the only thing they respond to. They will only respect someone stronger than them," I say with a smile, and unleash some of the power bubbling under my skin.

The thick-pile Persian rug beneath my feet begins to abrade away, tiny particles circling around me and my captive like a tornado. Then I really let it out, and the chaise behind me, and every single stick of furniture not nailed down moves as if pulled by a string, smashing against the closest wall.

"Trust me when I say, gentlemen, I'm stronger than you. Any questions?"

9

WEST—ONE MONTH LATER

I'D ALWAYS THOUGHT MY LIFE UP TO THIS POINT WAS AS BAD AS it could get. I figured nothing could be worse than my childhood and the gutter I crawled my way out of. I thought my father was the worst man I'd ever meet, and the level of his depravity and malice would forever go unsurpassed.

I had no idea.

I never made it out of that cell. Walter had no intention of listening to me or meeting with me for any other reason than to inflict pain. He paid me a visit in my lovely six-by-nine cell for the first time about a month ago.

And every day—every waking moment—is worse than the last.

He told me all about his visit with Evangeline, and I couldn't help but be proud of my Angel. My tiny, little pixie sure showed him. His nose had the obvious slant of a fresh break, and there were anywhere from ten to twenty small slices in the flesh of his cheeks, lips and forehead. I was proud—still am—but I paid the price.

Every single cut and broken bone, every slash and crunch, every single gasp of pain and drop of blood.

I paid.

I'm still paying.

He refuses to kill me, though. No, that would be too easy. It would let me off the hook, and Walter is having far too much fun. I know why I'm here. I'm a tool, a weapon, a chink in Evangeline's armor. They know how much she loves me, and I her. They know so much about her. Not from my own mouth, though. I have suffered absolute agony, and still I haven't said a peep.

But, I'm not the only prisoner here, and those prisoners don't love her like I do. Voyt and Kyle are two that I know of. In fact, their cells are on either side of mine. Voyt tried to get me out, tried to convince Walter that I was an asset to him. He had no idea what he was getting himself into.

My dungeon-mates don't know it yet, but I have a plan to get us out of here. I just need one little sliver of a chance, and we're bouncing out of this hell hole. Really, only one of us needs to get out, but I'm gunning for the three of us.

I refuse to leave a man behind.

My only respite is this cell, and as awful as it is, I'd rather be here. The torture is never inflicted here, only in the main chamber at the end of the corridor. That chamber has all the tools—pokers, blades, vices, racks, presses, manacles—all with the stench of old blood and the sweat of agony. But my respite never lasts very long. I can't remember the last time I ate anything, and it brings back memories of my childhood. The cold hunger in my belly, the wet chill that never seems to go away.

Then, my chance comes. The guards have never tried to get me out of my cell without incapacitating me first. Which is smart of them. Usually, they open a narrow slot in my door, slip the barrel of a gun through the gap in the steel and shoot me with a healthy dose of tranquilizer. It has happened enough, and I've been in this cell long enough, that I know the sounds heralding the shot. Tensing, readying myself for what I have to do, I try to keep my intentions off my face.

When the shot finally comes, I almost fail. The needle barely pricks my flesh before I catch it, stopping the dart from embedding into my belly. From experience, I know it takes a minute or two for the drugs to take effect, so when I pretend to pull the dart from my stomach, I know I have at least two minutes before they'll come in to get me. I relax my body slowly, ignoring the pain in my broken toes and shin, ignoring the slashes and bruises and seeping wounds, faking a drugged sleep better than I thought I'd be able to. I'm tired, and those pharmaceutically enhanced nap times have been the best sleep I've gotten here.

Too bad they're usually followed up by torture.

Two guards file into my cell, each taking an end and carry me down the corridor to the room I'm dreading. I dread, yet am thankful for this room. Whoever did the warding on my cell, failed to do the same level of warding on the torture chamber. I feel the magic in the air, and I have a sneaking suspicion I can travel out of that room. While my cell is damn near impenetrable, the room-of-pain has little pockets of un-warded space —hopefully, big enough for us to travel through.

That is *if* we can travel.

My transportation and I are the last to arrive to the party, and I peek through my eyelashes to survey the room. Voyt, Kyle, and another small form are uncon-scious and already manacled to wooden racks that look older than I am. A few torches dot the walls of the circular space, highlighting the tools of the torture trade, but keeping most of the area covered in inky shadow. Sharp hooks, dragon's tail rope darts, curved knives, vices with spiked barbs, and more all hang from pegs in the stone.

The guards drop me unceremoniously on the wooden rack, and I notice the four of us are positioned equidistantly apart almost as if we are the four points of a compass.

Not good. Really, really not good.

We have never all been here together, and the fact that we are arranged in such a way... this does not bode well for us.

Just then, a man strides into the room. He's mostly in shadow, staying to the dark edges of the room, but stops at the rack that points south—or what I think is south—where a very small form rests. The flames flicker just right, and I catch a glimpse of copper hair.

Nicola.

Oh. Shit.

No wonder they knew so much about us. I wonder how long she and Kyle have been here. Did they get him first? Her? And how in the hell did they sneak up on an Oracle for fuck's sake? I don't care if she's blind, the woman is a damn psychic.

I have too many questions and no way to get answers—no way to know anything but that we have to get out of here as soon as fucking possible.

The man leans down, whispering in her ear—his voice so low I can't make out a single word. Her unseeing eyes flash open, her head and shoulders rise off the wooden rack, her face so horrified she can't even speak. Nicola shakes her head violently, mouthing the word 'No' over and over again.

The man turns from her and goes to the rack to her left where Kyle is still unconscious. His face is visible now. Blond hair tops sharp and angular features, and his cold smile reminds me of Walter's so much this man must be an Emerson.

He pulls a wicked blade from a sheath at his belt and begins to remove Kyle's shirt. Once Kyle's chest is exposed, the man begins debating where to place the knife, asking Nicola where she would like her mate to be stuck in the sickest sing-song voice I have ever heard. He's beyond deranged and taking great joy in the hypothetical torture of her sleeping mate.

"Come on, Nikki. Tell me. The lung? The heart? Maybe the liver? How do you want your mate to die,

Nikki? How painful do you want it to be? Say yes, and I'll let him go. Say no one more time, and I'll make his death last days," he threatens as he runs the knife down Kyle's face. I don't blame her when she breaks down and reluctantly nods.

"No, Nic. Don't do this. Don't let them do that to you," Kyle groggily pleads, the cut of the knife rousing from his drugged slumber. He's yanking at his barbed steel manacles, drawing rivulets of blood with each pull.

"I have to. There's no other way," she rasps as she turns her head to face Kyle, her eyes unseeing, but her face pleading. He struggles to swallow, his head thudding on the rack and his body falters.

"Well, then. That was surprisingly easy," the man remarks, clapping his hands together as he walks to the center of the circle, raising his hands to the heavens and start to chant.

I don't know what's coming, but I need to get us out of here.

Now.

I spied Voyt's body lying untethered at the eastern point of the circle. He's feigning sleep, but I can tell by the rigid set of his shoulders, he's about to move. I cluck my tongue as quietly I can to get his attention, and he slowly turns his head to me. A silent conversation passes between us, and I knew we need to get Kyle and hopefully Nicola out of here before Crazy Ass Emerson can do whatever it is he's planning.

I nod to him to get Kyle while I go for Nicola. All the while Emerson is chanting, and some of the words he's using start to filter in my brain. They're Latin—only some long forgotten bastardized version that I haven't heard since childhood.

The words he's using filter through my poor knowledge of the language. Words like '*summon*' and '*return*' and '*death*'. And then it all comes clear. He's trying to summon a soul from the Otherside.

My head whips to Voyt, and I can tell he just put it together himself because the blood drains from his face. Then Nicola starts thrashing and screaming, her pained cries so loud they reverberate off the stone walls, echoing into a tortured tornado of agony. We don't wait, and travel to our respective charges, him much faster than me and it takes me a second to realize I'm more injured than I thought.

In the next second that passes, as I yell for Voyt to take Kyle and go, realizing all too quickly that I can't carry both Nicola and myself out of here.

And I won't leave her behind to suffer. Not like I suffered.

I don't see or hear the man behind me, but I do feel

the sharp sting of the dart embedding its way into my back.

Well, at least they got out, I think as the stone floor rushes up to meet my face.

WEST—1423—SCOTLAND

I woke up in my bed of old thatching before the light ever cracked across the sky. I had chores to do and a limited amount of time to do them. Father wanted things just so, and if I didn't get them done timely enough, I wouldn't be able to walk the next day.

My tunic and breeches were woefully inadequate for the winter weather, and my shoes were three steps past threadbare. The snow seeped into the holes in them as I trudged through it to gather water from the well and give the horses their daily drink. Having no coat, I shivered in the freezing air, but you'd better believe Father had one. I needed shoes and clothes and at the very least a sheepskin to keep me warm at night. At ten years old, I had long since forgotten what warmth felt like. I didn't even have enough food to put a dent in the hunger in my belly.

But Father did.

Father's bed was more than just thatching on the dirt floor of one of the outbuildings. His was in the house proper and was up off the ground in a wooden bedframe. He didn't have a dirt floor—he had slate. His mattress was filled with feathers and fresh straw, and his meals were more than scraps left over that I stole from the dogs and pigs.

I wasn't the only servant—and make no mistake, that's exactly what I was—I was just the only one he had fathered. A bastard child of a sadistic nobleman and the poor dairy maid he took as repayment of a debt—I was only slightly more important than pig shit on his boot heel. The other servants knew my place. I was less than nothing, an inconvenience. The only person who had ever loved me was my mother, but she'd died a rather painful death three winters ago.

I'd promised myself as soon as I could find a way out, I'd take it, but there have been plenty of chances, and I hadn't taken any of them. It felt wrong to leave when I feared humans so. I didn't know how to hide yet. I was a good twenty years until maturity and knew no family who would take me in.

And why would they?

My father ruled over this village of Wraiths. He was known to be an evil man—evil but cunning. No one would dare go against him, and at least here, I knew what to expect.

"Henry!" I heard my father's slurred voice shout, and I froze.

He so rarely called me by name. It was usually 'boy' or whatever horrible name he could come up with on that given day.

I searched my mind and was certain I did everything required of me. I fed and watered the horses, fed the pigs, gathered water for the house and mucked the stable.

But I forgot one crucial detail.

It didn't matter if I completed my chores or if I didn't. Some days, I would receive a beating anyway. Not just beatings. These were the worst forms of punishment. Broken bones, blood drawn. And he did things to me. Things I hope to never think of again. Things I'd never wish on my worst enemy.

I took a deep breath and went to face my father, but staying to the shadows so I could see him first. I peered around a hay cart, and my belly dropped. It was barely past midday, and he was already drunk on mulled wine. Drunk or sober, it didn't matter, he was still mean as a snake, but drunk was invariably worse.

"HENRY!" he roared again, and I knew, I just knew my time on this earth was up.

He held a knife—a shiny silver dagger I'd seen him carry before. Usually, it hung in a small scabbard at his belt, and as far as I knew, he'd only been without it once. He'd lost it in a game of chance, but I'd heard the other servants say he murdered the man who won it from him—rather brutally—to get it back.

"Y-yes, Sir?" I said, the small act of calling him 'sir' instead of 'my lord' was an act of defiance, but I hated how my voice wobbled. I was never permitted to call him Father, even though everyone knew he was mine. We looked just alike—same dark hair, same tall stature, same green eyes. Our noses, our chins, our cheeks— they all matched.

I was my father—just in miniature.

I could tell my face irked him. It was in his expression every time he looked at me.

"Did you take this book?" he said, brandishing the leather-bound journal like a weapon. I'd hidden it in a secret nook in the stable—well, not so secret anymore —and read through it most nights. I'd pilfered it from my mother's things years ago. Father had taken all of her possessions from me when she died. I had nothing from her until I stole that journal back before he could burn it.

My mother—unlike many of the other servants— knew how to read and write, and taught me at a very young age. I knew what was in that journal. I knew every secret and every wrong doing my father had orchestrated over the last ten years. I knew the pain my mother endured. And I knew what she faced before he killed her.

Painfully. He drew out her punishment for days before there was nothing left to her. Before her poor body just couldn't take another moment.

But that journal was my ticket to freedom—as soon as I could muster the courage. And he had my ticket in his filthy, drunkard hands.

"Answer me, boy!" he roared, but he didn't need an answer.

He needed an excuse. An excuse to kill me just like my mother. Now he had one.

I wasn't expecting him to throw the book down and charge me. My only saving grace was his drunken state —it helped me avoid the flashing steel in his hand. Otherwise, the dagger he held just a moment ago would have ended up in my belly instead of in the dirt where it laid between us. He lunged for it first, but stumbled over his own feet, landing on all fours in the muck.

I knew he wasn't going to stop. He was going to keep reaching for that dagger until it made its home in my gut. I debated saving myself until he reached for it again, and then it wasn't in my control whether or not I was going to grab for the knife—I plucked it from the dirt before his awful fingers could close over the carved silver hilt.

"You give my dagger back to me, boy," he ordered as he climbed to his feet.

His face had clarity to it, he was either no longer drunk or had sobered up enough to know I'd protect myself if I had to. Like my mother couldn't.

"No," I whispered.

"Henry Carmichael Weston, you give me the dagger back right now!" he roared as he lunged, staggering at the last possible second and impaling himself on the blade.

My only thought was on the fact that he called me by my full name—the name my mother gave me as a slight to him because it carried a part of him that he refused to acknowledge. The part that named him my father. I hadn't even been sure he knew my full name until then.

Father lurched backward off of the blade, but the damage was already done. Dark red blood flowed from the wound in his chest, pouring down his pale brocade tunic and velvet breeches all the way down to the buckles on his boots. He lost his feet then, his knees hitting the ground first.

In my ten-year-old brain, I was still stuck on the

name—my mind refusing to process the death of my tormentor.

His face turned a sick shade of gray, the blood that used to fill it flooded from him in great gushes. Then he fell, face-first into the muck, still and silent as only the dead can be.

"That's not my name anymore," I said to his back, and those were the last words I spoke for a very long time.

10

VOYT

Traveling injured is not my favorite thing in the world to do. It isn't even in the top ten. Or twenty. Or three million. Traveling injured is taking an already agonizing activity and making it black-out-from-pain awful. Three weeks in Walter's care is probably what Hell feels like. It makes me never ever want to fuck up so royally that I have to go to Hell, because I think I'd rather intentionally set myself on fire.

It's my own fault. I should have been better at the stealth. I should have been able to talk these guys around, and if I couldn't do that, then I had to figure out what the game was and see what I could do to stop it since West was stuck in that cell because of me. I had a week. One single week to try and get as much info as I could to give to Evangeline.

I failed and got myself caught.

Now that I'm out, I have no idea what I am supposed to do other than tell Evangeline everything. And pray she doesn't kill me.

Jesus Christ on a crutch, Kyle is the heaviest person I have ever carried, and I pray I never have to do it again. It took me three tries to get myself and Kyle to Mena and fifteen to reach that doorbell once I got us to her front porch. I'm just lucky I remembered where she was looking to buy a house, or I would be worse than screwed.

I'd be dead.

It's freezing this high up the mountain, and given the fact that I'm wearing a pair of three-weeks-long soiled jeans and nothing else does absolutely zilch in the way of making this any better. The door opens after what seems like an eternity on this damn porch and Asher sees Kyle and immediately drags him inside.

What the am I, chopped liver?

It's hard for me to talk and has been for some time. I'd been screaming quite a bit over the last few weeks, and the last time I screamed it felt like I was swallowing glass. I haven't tried talking, and I don't want to. I've had enough pain thank you very much.

It takes me ten more tries to reach the damn doorbell from my slumped position on rust-colored porch planks. They're half-hearted swats at the freaking thing, but I can't bring myself to try harder. My light is going out, but I need to figure out a way to tell them what happened.

I need to figure out where West went.

I need to... I need to...

When the door opens again, Mena is the one to grab me under my armpits and drag me into the foyer of a modest, but elegant mountain house. But the foyer floor is freezing—still warmer than the frigid temperature outside—and I need to tell her...

When her burning hot hand touches my shoulder, I flinch away from the warmth. My body so cold it can't handle even the slight heat of her hand. But then the warmth floods through me—easing aches I'd long forgotten about, loosening my throat and mending the awful tearing of my vocal chords. Her enormous power is not enough—not right now anyway—to heal all of it, and the ease of so many aches and so long without sleep and nourishment takes its toll, and I speak the first words that have passed my lips in weeks.

"Get Evangeline," I say, my voice odd to my own ears, and that is all I am able to get out before my consciousness dims into nothing and I pass out right there on that cold fucking tile.

MENA

Not one, but two Wraiths passed out in my foyer.

Fuck a damn duck.

"Rally everyone. Bring them here. Can you call Aurelia? She and Rhys can drive over. I don't like her traveling in her condition," I tell Asher before he even has to ask. I love when I don't need him to ask, I can just read the expression on his face. It helps when the shit hits the fan.

Kinda like right about now.

I get a nod and a brief but scorching kiss before he smokes out from the room, off to get the rest of the family here.

I loathe that I am not able to communicate in this modern world. There has to be something I can do that won't A) burn the house down or B) fry every electronic component this side of the Colorado River. Maybe if I bleed enough healing, I could do something... The thought has merit, and it couldn't hurt Kyle or Voyt. By the looks of them, they need it.

Kyle is the better off of the two, but not by very much. The slice in his cheek started closing as soon as I touched him, so the loss of consciousness is probably the dire need for sleep. If there were anyone who knows what prolonged torture is like, it is me.

Both shirtless, it is easy to see that the starvation torture tactic was favored which just pisses me off. I've never met Kyle before, but I can tell he used to be something. His height is probably closer to seven feet than six and by the look at his bare feet, he'd need a shoe the size of a damn boat. Jet black hair and beard that has gone long past mountain-man and straight into hermit in the woods land. For such a large man, he shouldn't be as emaciated as he is. I'll get Aurelia started on that as soon as she gets here.

Voyt, however, is in a bad way. The slight beard on his face and the fact that I just saw him three weeks ago tells me he was interred for a much shorter time than Kyle, but the damage done to him is significant. Voyt had much less meat to lose, and he looks like a skeleton. His already sharp cheekbones have turned knife-edged, and when he spoke, I could tell his time screaming must have been considerable.

I remember screaming. I remember ripping my vocal chords to shit but being unable to stop screaming anyway. I fucking hate evil people.

His skin is nearly freezing, and I need to move them both from the cold tile and get them somewhere warm.

I take Voyt first because he has so much less meat on his bones and needs the warmth first. I'm so happy no one is here to see me pick him up and cradle him like a baby in my arms as I carry him to the right side of the sectional in the living room. I would hate for anyone to see him in this state, and I would hate for anyone to make fun of him.

No one knows better than me the power you lose. The shame you feel at not only being caught in a spider's web but all the things you begged for, all the things you promised the Fates you'd do to get out, all the things you swore you'd never do just to be free. Those are the wounds that never heal. Those are the ones that when even the slightest offhand insult can cause a world of hurt.

And I can't have that for these men.

I pick up Kyle next and due to his size and considerable weight—even emaciated as he is—I need to fireman carry him to the couch. Once I have them positioned as comfortably as I can, I scurry to find our thick mink blankets and pillows. Then I start a fire. I'm sweating and the house is nearly sweltering, but they need it. Starting a fire is easy for me, obviously, but it took some time to control my Fireskin enough to not have it run all over my body. Aurelia knew how to control hers before we were even at maturity. Controlling anything other than my Aegis as a child was something I lacked.

Aurelia and Rhys are the first to arrive, and since they live less than ten minutes away, this isn't surprising. She barely bundled up to the elements outside, wearing only black leggings and a thin sapphire, open-weave sweater tunic over a black camisole and I give Rhys my best 'are you kidding me' glare. Mostly because she's not wearing any shoes or socks.

"I know. I tried," he says as he holds up his arm which is laden down with her parka, thick, woolen socks, and boots.

That's it.

"Aurelia Corrine Constantine, I swear to all that is holy if you do not start making sure your health is priority number one, I'm going to make you regret it! You. Are. Pregnant. You know it. Rhys knows it. Everyone knows it. Phoenixes don't get sick. We don't get the flu or food poisoning or car sickness for pity's sake. There is no other reason you'd be throwing up so much. Stop being in denial and accept the fact that you are carrying a child and need to tailor your behaviors accordingly. Now, put on the socks," I yell, finishing my tirade on a scream loud enough to rattle the windows and wake the dead.

Her surprised face tells me she didn't even consider

this a possibility, but she holds her hand out to Rhys for the socks, unseeingly sitting on the closest armchair to slip them on her feet.

Mission accomplished.

I go over to her, crouching down in front of her chair to see her face better. I grasp her shoulders until her eyes come to me, and when they finally meet mine they are filled with tears.

"You're sure?" she says in a small voice, and it is a voice laced with hope.

"Yes, big sister. I'm sure. But we can have Ian check if you need him too."

"That would be great," she says nodding.

I feel her body draw on my Aegis a bit, not a lot, just a tiny bit, and it hits me. She's tired and stressed, and this little pull tells me more about her health than any silly blood test or sonogram would.

"And I don't know how to break this to you, but I'm pretty sure you're having twins," I whisper lowly, but not low enough.

"What?" Rhys breathes before his eyes roll back in his head, and he falls out, luckily landing on the plush area rug and barely avoiding the hand-carved solid oak end table Asher carved last week.

Three men down.

Fuck a damn duck.

II

EVAN

I'm going to lose my mind. Nope, I'm sure I've already lost it.

I'm standing in the middle of Mena and Asher's new house with my hands on my hips waiting for someone to start talking sense. Voyt and Kyle are finally awake and propped up on several pillows on the wide-cushioned dark, buttery leather sectional. They are shoveling in heaping spoonfuls of Aurelia's broccoli-cheddar-bacon-chicken soup, and as soon as she sees the bottom of their bowls, she whisks them away before they can ask for a refill. She has gone into full-scale mother hen mode, and I know why.

In this room, I am one of the few who haven't

undergone torture. I'm one of the lucky ones and it burns in the back of my throat that these men were treated this way. That they were hurt on my watch. It also makes me wish I would have ripped Walter's throat out when I had the chance.

But the more they try and talk me into going to get West, the more I want to scream. The more I hear why he was doing what he was doing, the more I want to slap the shit out of him. In the back of my mind, I know he did this out of love.

I know this. I do. *Maybe.*

But it just shows how little he valued what I had to say. How little he trusted me to know what was best. How little he believed I could handle this throne on my own.

"He was doing it to keep you safe, Evangeline. That's why he wouldn't mate you," Voyt pleads, his voice a sharp gravel he didn't have before.

"No. He did this because he didn't trust me. He never has," I whisper the painful truth, and it is the most honest thing I've ever said about him. Because if he wanted to wait, why did he just say that? Why didn't he tell me why instead of just changing the subject or putting me off?

It's not like I'm some ring-starved co-ed begging their boyfriend of three months to pop the question. I'm his mate. I'm who the Fates chose for him.

But he didn't trust me with the truth. Not really.

West Carmichael has never trusted me, and that pill is the hardest to swallow. Never. No matter that I gave him everything in me. My thoughts, my dreams, my ideas, my body, my love.

Everything I had to give, and now there's nothing left.

"He did. I swear. He just wanted you safe," Rhys' voice rumbles behind me.

"I didn't need him to keep me safe. I can do that for myself. I just needed him to trust. Just once know that I could do it myself. You can't love someone you don't trust, and this is once again proof that he never loved me."

"Are you just going to let him rot?" Voyt asks incredulously, ripping the blanket off his legs and moving to stand.

Aurelia nips it in the bud before he can put a hand to the cushion to heft himself up, leveling him with a look that could peel the paint off a car. She's not letting him go anywhere.

"No, she isn't going to let him rot. Sit your skinny ass down and eat some bread," she says handing him a chunk of fresh sourdough.

The smell of it must be good because he begrudgingly takes and bite while giving her a petulant look.

"All this bitching about West is not getting me my mate back," Kyle's pissed off growl resonates through the room.

His face is gaunt behind months of beard growth and filth, but his eyes are bright and shining. He has hope for her, and my sad eyes just piss him off.

"She's not dead. My Nicola is a fighter. No way is she going to let that bitch win. We might have disrupted them. He might not have had enough sacrifices for the spell. She might be okay. She has to be. I'd feel it. I would. I'd feel it if she were gone," his voice frantic with blind hope.

He doesn't even believe himself, though, because this big bear of a man breaks—great gasping howls of agony rip up from his throat. Cam puts a comforting hand on his shoulder in a show of support, and it just proves once again that Cam is someone who knows loss.

"She did it for me, you know? That slimy fucker said he was going to kill me, and she knew. She knew he meant it. That's the only reason she'd do that. The only reason she'd allow it. She's been watching them torture me for months. But I told her. I told her I would take it. I would take it to my end if it meant she didn't let them put that fucking monster in her. But they were going to kill me... I told her no. I told her no. Why did she do that?" he asks, and I know the answer.

Because she loved him.

If Nicola didn't survive it, how could West? They said he was the worst off of the lot. He could be gone...

The thought runs through my brain, and the stab of fiery pain rips through my chest. He may have never loved me, but I still love him despite my best efforts. No, I won't let him rot. Whether he loves me or not, I still love him. That will just have to be enough to pull his ass out of the flames.

"We'll get them back, Kyle. I'll do everything in my power to get them back. I swear to you. I will," I promise as I kneel down in front of his perch on the couch.

"This might make me the pragmatic asshole of the group, but the question has to be asked. Have they passed? Because I'm not risking the Queen's life for a dead man, I don't care if I have to hog tie you and stuff you in a closet," Aidan says, his eyes boring into mine with enough force that I know he means it.

It doesn't matter if he means it or not, and it doesn't matter if West is alive or dead. Walter Emerson is going to die tonight, that is for damn certain. I flash my fangs at Aidan, so he knows I don't take kindly to his threat.

To help stave off the fight that is about to break out in the middle of the living room, Aurelia butts in.

"I haven't seen them pass if that helps," she says.

"Good. We're going. Get your shit and let's go," I order and almost everyone starts moving—including Kyle.

"Whoa, whoa, whoa there, hoss. You're going nowhere. Sit your big ass down," Aurelia tells him, crossing the room to put a hand on his shoulder, holding him down and he's having a hard time not throwing it off of him and leaving. His face isn't petulant—it is lethal.

A feral growl rips up Rhys' throat, but Aurelia lays a calming hand on his chest holding him off as she turns back to Kyle.

"Don't look at me like that, mister. I can't go either."

"Why can't you go?" I ask, hearing the thread of panic in my own voice. I need her. I need her with me. I need her so much right now.

"I'm knocked up, kiddo. I love you more than anyone, but I'm not risking my children for anyone or anything. Sorry, baby girl," Aurelia explains, her eyes pleading me to understand.

And I do. She wouldn't ever admit it, but losing her child was the worst day of her life. She would have gladly taken torture, death, anything. And now that she...

"Wait, what? Pregnant? Child-*ren*?" I ask baffled.

I knew she was sick, but I just thought... I don't know what I thought, but pregnancy never crossed my mind.

"Evidently, Phoenixes don't get sick. Ever. The only reason I'd be throwing up is if I either broke a bone—which I haven't—or if I'm knocked up. I have it on good authority I am expecting twins. You missed it when Rhys passed out. It was hilarious," she explains, smiling this beaming grin.

Huh. My bestie is having babies. I love it.

"That... makes sense," I say, nodding, a smile stretching across my face so fast I think it might crack and I look to Mena. "We're sharing auntie duties. I don't want to hear any guff, got it?" I inform her pointing so she knows I mean business.

My comment is met with an insolent '*no shit, Sherlock*' look that is similar to Aurelia's, it makes me smile. But it fades as soon as the problem at hand comes back to me. West. Nicola. *Iva.*

"Glad we got that cleared up. Plan B. Who's coming?" Cam says irritably.

"Not me," Rhys pipes up. "If I get a scratch, she gets

a scratch. If I die, I lose both her and the babies. I'm not risking it."

Rhys has been her shadow, watching her with more than his usual intensity, and it is starting to make sense. He never thought he would get that with her. Now that the dream is within reach, he'll do anything not to lose it.

I don't blame him, but that leaves us two warriors down. Myself, Aidan, Cam, Carver, Ian, and hopefully Mena and Asher are helping.

"Everyone else besides Voyt, Kyle, Aurelia & Rhys is coming, right? Anyone else bowing out?" I ask looking around the room. Mena meets my eyes, and I didn't realize that her expressions are nearly identical to her twin's. This one says *'I'm ready to fuck shit up.'* Fates, I love these women.

Voyt and Kyle give us a rundown of what they knew of the layout and security measures, and then we load up with the scary amount of blades, firearms, body armor and ammunition stocked in Mena and Asher's basement.

But I don't know if it's enough.

I already don't like this plan, and we're five seconds into it.

Voyt told us all about the cameras, motion sensors and personnel floating around the Emerson house. He did not, however, tell us about the warding, and this place is sealed up tighter than an alligator's asshole.

We are a mile out from the house, and to a human's eye, there is nothing here. Even I'm having a hard time focusing on the space beyond the ward, and I assume that's the idea. The ward is barely visible, but it doesn't need to be. I'm certain every single member of the Ethereal can feel it. It was like they were either begging to be found or shouting to back off.

Either way, I don't know how we can break it without a Witch, and I don't have one of those in my pocket.

I suppose it is possible he didn't know, and Kyle's input wasn't helpful at this level due to the fact he didn't come here of his own free will, and rather, he was dragged here while unconscious by people he never saw.

"Pfft," Mena scoffs at the barrier. "I could bust this in my damn sleep, but I might as well take out the cameras, motion sensors and electricity while I'm at it, so you need to skedaddle for a minute."

"Nothing doing, Princess. We have no clue who's

out here. We're not going anywhere," Asher counters taking the words right out of my mouth.

Good man. Mena looks to me to get another girl's opinion, but I'm already shaking my head.

"Fine, but if you see me start to slip, get the hell out of here. Killing the good guys is not on my list of tonight's activities."

"Sure, thing," I tell her, and I get *'the eyebrow'* in response as she eyes me skeptically. "Seriously," I promise, and the lot of us—at her urging—back up at least a hundred feet.

When the light show begins, I think nothing of it. I'm waiting for the ward to break, waiting to get to him. Waiting to bring him home.

So when Mena screams, it comes as to worst kind of shock.

Because we are surrounded.

Because this was a trap.

And my blind need to get West back may have killed us all.

12

EVAN

IF I MAKE IT OUT OF HERE, IF I EVER SEE WEST CARMICHAEL again, I'm slapping the shit out of him. This thought runs on loop in my brain as I take another head shot, watching my bullet bore through the skull of another Guardian. I hate doing this. I hate taking life, but I hope I'm at least making a dent—cutting out the cancer that is infecting our race. The fact that they're closing in on us like the tightening of a noose does wonders to keep the guilt at bay.

They were silent as the grave when they surrounded us, likely lying in wait and ready for us to arrive. That's the problem with them having an Oracle at their disposal and us having no one. They can see ahead. They can know, plan.

I should have thought to have Aurelia on coms.

Or at least Rhys since she has a bad habit of frying electronics, but I didn't think ahead. I didn't think of anything but getting to West, and that stupid lack of planning got us here. I swear, if I lose anyone, I'll never forgive myself.

And I'll never forgive him.

For Wraiths, it is easy to tell who is evil and who is not. The evil ones make us hungry—ravenous really—so hungry we can barely control it. The more power you possess, the hungrier you get. It is why Revenants are such a problem. Sometimes, anger and hate drives us, and when that happens, the hunger takes over, and it's just a hop, skip and jump to heart-eating crazytown. It turns normal, level-headed, reasonable individuals into flesh-hungry sociopaths. This is why balance is so hard.

Because evil souls are tasty.

The ones that don't feel as appetizing—the ones that maybe, someday, could be saved—I shoot in the kneecap instead of the head. Fighting my urge to consume—the urge to finally feel full—I keep going until I run out of ammo for the Glock and realize I may be just the tiniest bit screwed.

I'm separated from everyone else, and although I can hear them fighting, I can't see them through the trees. What I can see are four Guardians eyeing me with the smug indifference of men who think they've already won.

The eight of us against an army. Who thought that was a good plan? Oh, that's right. Me.

I'm an idiot.

I pull a tri-dagger from its sheath on my right hip and plunge it into the chest of the closest Guardian.

Heal from that, you bastard.

I'd never used the tri-dagger before, and despite its weight, I have to admit, it is handy. Handy and deadly— a triangular, oscillating shank with venting holes bored into the center to prevent suction. I knew I'd only use it if I meant to kill, and as much as I hate taking life, as much as I hate the stain to my soul, I choose to live.

These bastards aren't going to stand between West and me.

As I rip the dagger out of the first Guardian's chest, I pull the small rapier out of my back sheath, adjust to an overhand grip and make an economical slash to the second's neck. The blade slides through his windpipe like melted butter, and I have to give it to Aidan, when he said he made sure it was the sharpest it could get, he was right. The third and fourth Guardians travel to me in rage. I can't blame them per se—I did just take out two of their buddies in less than a second—but their double-teaming isn't convenient, to say the least. When they pop up right in front of me, I get the sinking feeling in my gut that I might be not long for this world.

Two whole months as Queen. That has to be a record.

An arc of lightning passes right in front of my face, simultaneously hitting a Guardian in the chest and blowing me off my feet. I'm not sure if I should be grateful I'm not dead or pissed Mena put me on my ass. I'll go with grateful at the moment because living and flat on my ass is better than dead any day of the week.

I make it to my feet in time to watch Mena grab the last Guardian by the throat and shock him into dust.

Note to self, do not piss this woman off.

"You all right?" she asks as she touches my shoulder, most likely checking for injuries. I've noticed she does this more now that she can control her Aegis better.

"I'm good, just got the wind knocked out of me," I return glancing around to check for threats.

"All the Guardians have been neutralized for the time being. I have to break this ward. I tried to have Ash get Aurelia on coms, and there is so much juju flying around here, I bet you money I couldn't even get a damn compass to work around it. If they have working electricity inside it, I'd be surprised," she informs me.

"What about our guys? Everyone okay?" I ask because ward or not, West or not, I need to know about my people.

"Bumps and bruises. Nothing major. Let's get the ward busted and get your man before they decide to send reinforcements."

"Agreed," I say, sheathing my dagger and grabbing her hand to travel the two hundred or so feet to the ward instead of walking it.

"Thanks for the lift," she says as she bumps me with her hip, half to get me out of the way and half as a thanks. I back up a bit and feel a hand on my shoulder. Cam is right behind my left shoulder, and his face is part apologetic, part proud, and part thankful I'm alive. None of the men in my life are what could be considered talkers—their facial expressions doing the speaking for them—so I've become an expert at reading faces.

I feel someone at my right, and I don't need to look to know it is Aidan, but I do to see what his face has to say. It is easy to read—it says I will be on you like white on rice, so don't try anything funny.

I nod and turn back to Mena, watching as she throws bolt after bolt of lightning from her fingers at the enormous barrier. When that doesn't work, she walks right up to the edge and places her palms on the slightly shimmering dome-like spell—giving it the full dose of her juice. The ward busts in an instant, but Mena wavers a moment before plopping down on her ass in the leaves.

"I just need a minute," she says as Asher cradles her in his arms.

"I'm not sure what kind of time we have, Princess. I need you to try and stand for me, babe," Asher tells her and she struggles to her feet.

"Try to get Rhys on coms. I have a feeling we're going to need a Seer for this shit. There is bad juju going on here."

"I fucking hate Witches," Carver says from behind us as he plugs his earpiece into his phone and dials Rhys.

"You think you could get your wife to look out for us here? I've already almost died once this year, and I have to say, I've lost my taste for it," Carver says by way of greeting before he nearly drops the phone as his eyes go wide. Even in the near blackness of the dim, I can see his caramel face go gray.

"She said she can't see anything. All she sees is blackness," Carver croaks, his eyes filling.

"What?" I breathe, and it feels like someone has ripped the heart from my chest. I can't lose him too. I can't...

Before anyone can stop me, I move, traveling to the

front steps of this ostentatious mansion. I lift my foot and kick the flimsy fucking door open. I met with nothing.

No sound. No lights. No people.

Nothing.

My heart wants to drop and soar at the same time. Maybe the blackness Aurelia sees isn't death. Maybe he isn't gone. Maybe the blackness she sees is just the dark.

Please, please, let it just be the dark, I think as I step carefully through the ground level, making my way to the basement dungeon based on the directions Voyt gave me. He only had one request—if I saw a blonde woman named Claire, that I take her with us. He promised she was a good woman, but I'm hesitant to follow his request. I suppose I'll just have to judge her myself. If she's even here.

I make it to the bottom of the ricketiest staircase ever made when I feel a presence to my left. Moving before I think, I stop myself from embedding the tri-dagger in Cam's throat at the absolute last second, earning him a nick to his Adam's apple.

The look I give him tells him I'm not sorry, and I move past him down a moldy stone corridor lined on both sides by vault-like cell doors.

I smell death. So much death it makes my stomach turn. There are no evil souls here, only innocents, and by the twist in my gut, they feel young—not even to maturity.

I can't stand it, the blankness in my brain wants control, so I keep it at bay by turning the doors to dust. The first door to my right contains the remains of a dead Shifter—still in his shifted form, I can't tell his age, but I know he was some sort of big cat. Moving to the left one, I find the remains of a Warlock who couldn't be more than fifteen human years old.

The bile rises, but I won't stop until I find him. I find another Shifter and the body of a Witch child no more than eight. The tears come, and I don't stop them.

When the next two cells turn up empty, it is a relief, but then again, it isn't. Every cell is either empty or full of death. I don't want to check the rest, fearing the death I still feel crawling against my skin. I hesitate before I dissolve the next door.

What if he's gone when I find him? I shouldn't have sent him away. I shouldn't have let him go. *Please. Please, please, please don't let him be dead.*

My hands are shaking when I place them on the door. The solid metal door abrades away bit by bit, slower than the others because I have a feeling I know what is behind this door, and if he's gone I almost don't want to know.

But it isn't West's large form I see on the cold, steel

cot, but a crumpled blonde woman—and she's breathing.

"Mena! One of them is alive!" I yell back to the hallway.

She's a Wraith, certainly, and she's unconscious, huddled into a tiny ball on the cot, her arms wrapped tight around her bent legs even in sleep. Her face is bruised so horribly one of her eyes looks as if it would stay closed even if she were awake. Her nose assuredly broken and still dripping blood, and her fingernails are bleeding and jagged.

Mena joins me in the cell and immediately grabs her hand. I watch as the bruises fade from the prisoner's battered face, and the swelling deflates to reveal her beauty. A few more seconds and her eyelids flutter open. When she sees Mena and me, she flinches back.

"Wh-who are you?" she asks, her voice trembling.

"I'm Evangeline Black, your Queen, and this is Mena Constantine, leader of the Phoenixes. Who are you?"

"C-Claire. My name is Claire," she whispers.

"I was hoping you'd say that. Voyt asked us to bring you with us. Is that all right with you?" I ask her gently.

I won't take her if she doesn't want to come, but I don't expect an objection. Her frantic, shaky nod confirms it.

"We're looking for West. Have you seen him?" I ask her, my voice breaking.

She shakes her head no and says, "I haven't seen him today. I'm so sorry, but if he's here, he might be in the chamber at the end of the corridor. But... Be careful," her voice halts as her tears spill over. "Bad things happen in there."

I try to bolt from the room, but Cam stops me.

"Not this time, darling girl. Let one of us go. You've done enough."

"No. It has to be me. I have to see for myself."

Of all the doors in the hallway, this is the only one that is unlocked, and that fact is the scariest of them all. No one wants to go to this room, I know it in my gut.

And after what happens here, no one is able to leave on their own steam. Claire is right.

Bad things do happen here.

Blood is pooled underneath a wooden rack that is one of four set in a circle. And on it is a man... If he weren't the other half of my soul, I'd never be able to recognize what's left of him. Even from here I can barely make out the features of his face. His body emaciated, his skin mottled green and purple.

And the blood. So much blood. I can't...

I travel to him, unable to walk the thirty feet from the door to the northernmost rack.

"West. Baby? Help me! Somebody help me!" I scream searching his neck and wrists for a pulse.

I can't find one.

A pair of hands gently pull me away as Mena and Ian work on him—trying to put Humpty Dumpty back together again.

I don't know if they can.

All I can do is hope.

13

WEST—1969—BETHEL, NY

IF I WATCHED ONE MORE HIPPIE ASSHOLE OFFER A SMOKE TO my woman, I couldn't be held responsible for what I did next. I didn't know when I started thinking of her as my woman. That's a lie. I knew exactly when it was. It was the first time I heard her speak. I'd heard her sing so many times before—a huskily haunting voice so beautiful it would put an angel to shame—but the first time I heard her speak...

I was lost, and I was found all at the same time. It was then that she became my Angel.

But my Angel was a pain in my ass. Of all the places we could be, of all the things could have been doing, we were standing in a field in the midst of hundreds of thousands of shirtless hippies. At least the music was good.

My Angel was in a lacy white dress with wilted daisies woven through her pale, curly locks. Her feet were bare—against my insistence that she put on some damn shoes—and she was dancing to the supreme guitar strains of Santana. It was the second day of the festival, and we had worked out an agreement. If she agreed not to sleep here in this mass of people, I would be happy to let her come back until it ended.

The real story was I couldn't stop her if she wanted to go, but if I didn't hold her too tight, if I didn't try to keep her in a cage, she would always tell me where she was going. Most of the time, she didn't like for me to be too close. She said I was too serious and made her feel like there was a noose around her neck choking the life out of her. That admission damn near broke my heart.

I never wanted to hurt her, never wanted to drown her. But that is what I was doing. Because I couldn't keep her. I couldn't disrespect John that way.

It was a flimsy excuse at best.

John most likely wouldn't mind, and Olivia surely wouldn't. Olivia would love for me to be her daughter's mate if it meant those rich jerks from the head families wouldn't weasel their way into her heart and into being King.

If there were a real noose, those pompous suitors would be it—they would want her to be proper and quiet. My Angel is anything but proper and couldn't be quiet even if you taped her mouth shut. But her constant talking meant I didn't have to talk at all. She did the bulk of it, and if I couldn't get by with grunts and nods, then I used silence.

It's worked for forty years, so why ruin it? If it ain't broke...

I'd do anything to keep her from knowing—from feeling the pull I feel. Anything to keep her from the wanting. There are so many reasons to keep her away from me.

I'm not a good man. It wasn't just my chosen profession, my past, or my lineage—they were all factors, absolutely—it was that I couldn't make myself leave her. I couldn't bring myself to tell John he needed to reassign me. I couldn't leave her in the hands of someone else.

Someone who wouldn't love her like I did. Someone who wouldn't treat her like the precious woman she was. Someone who wouldn't understand that she needed music like she needed breath, or that she had an unhealthy obsession with organizing things, or that she didn't consume nearly as much as she should.

I've followed her every single day for the last sixty-three years—mostly in the shadows and unbeknownst to my charge—making sure she was safe. I know more about her than anyone. I know that underneath all of her frenetic energy, despite the fact that she flits around like a hummingbird of smiles and light, she is probably the saddest person I have ever met.

She feels guilty—over something which is no more her fault than the color of the sky. She wouldn't blame an animal for snapping when wounded, or rain causing a flood, or the lightning causing a fire, so why she blames herself for losing control when she was in imminent danger is beyond me.

San Francisco was an accident. Nothing more or less, and I didn't blame her—not many did—but she still blamed herself. It was easy to see the lengths she went to not to lose control—only consuming little bits here and there so her body stayed tired. Then, she would run herself ragged, flitting about doing things for everyone she knew—helping, giving more and more of herself until there was nothing left.

So, no, I didn't want to cage her. I wanted her free. I wanted her safe. I wanted her to be mine.

But I wasn't going to get what I wanted—I wasn't going to keep her good soul with my tainted one.

Evangeline killed by accident. I killed on purpose.

And as I watched this beautiful pixie shine her light

in the throng of concertgoers I vowed to myself she'd never be mine.

WEST—1987—LONDON, ENGLAND

I'd lost her. I never had her in the first place, but I'd lost her all the same. She was tired of waiting for me. Tired of my silence. Tired of feeling the pull and getting nothing in return. Make no mistake—she felt it. It didn't matter that I tried my best to avoid speaking around her. I figured that if I didn't speak, she wouldn't know about the bond, but I failed in that endeavor about a decade ago.

She went on a date tonight.

The first date she's ever been on, at least to my knowledge—and the twist to my heart was unbearable. She wouldn't choose me over him, this pale-headed suitor with the nice clothes and even nicer car. Why would she? I have done nothing in these some eighty years to dissuade her.

Here I stood—in the rain no less—like a pathetic sack of shit waiting to get my heart ripped up a little more. He took her to a decent restaurant, a new Moroccan place that opened up last year. He pulled out her chair, opened her door, he was polite.

I wanted to murder him on sight.

I hated where we were living. I hated that we were so far from John and Olivia. I hated the rain and gray skies and cold weather. But it didn't stop me from agreeing that she needed a change.

My Angel was withering away. I thought keeping my vow would keep her safe, but...

It had been months since the last time she consumed a soul, and it was starting to show. She looked painfully gaunt, her cheeks hollow, her collarbone prominent despite the thick sweaters she wore. But I didn't know what to do, so I agreed to move across the world.

Still, she refused to consume.

Evangeline lived quiet here, managing an art gallery where her best friend's paintings regularly made an appearance. John has received roughly a dozen calls and updates from Aurelia about my Angel. It was good she had Aurelia—someone to talk to when she stopped talking to me. Someone else to care for her. I didn't even have to meet her to know Aurelia Constantine cared deeply for my Angel.

But John was worried, and Olivia was concerned enough that Aurelia kept her updated with daily phone calls.

But me? I was beside myself. Scared out of my mind for so many reasons.

Should I leave her be?

Should I butt into her date and take her away from this place?

Should I just get over myself and kiss her?

Evangeline wasn't getting any better. How much longer could she go before the damage was irreversible?

I watched them dine through the window, the barest hint of a smile passed her lips, quickly marred by a frown when she met my eyes through the glass. Oh, she was mad.

They ate their meals in tense silence and parted ways at the door of the restaurant. She waited impatiently for him to get into the low-slung car parked on the street and drive away before stomping across the street to me.

She was pissed, but I didn't care. There was a life to her that had been missing these last few years. So when she opened her mouth to yell at me for whatever reason she had to do so, I couldn't help myself.

I closed the few feet that separated us, wrapped an arm around her waist, fitted her small, firm body to mine, and kissed her with everything in me. Whatever she was about to say, whatever tirade she planned in those tense minutes while she waited for her date to end, died on her tongue as I met it with mine. I tangled my fingers in the thick curls of her hair and breathed her in—tasting her sweetness, her light—until I couldn't breathe anymore.

"You going out with that fucker again?" I asked, but I knew she wouldn't before she shook her head no.

"Why would I waste my time on anyone who wasn't you?" she asked by way of explanation.

I answered her with my mouth over hers, stealing both of our breaths as the warm, slick slide of her tongue met mine. I couldn't tell if she climbed me or if my hands moved of their own accord, but before I knew it, her pert little bottom was in my palms and her legs were wrapped around my waist.

I was soaked to the skin from the winter downpour, but I wasn't cold—not with this beautiful woman in my arms. Then I no longer felt the pelting of the rain and knew we'd moved. Once again, I wasn't sure if I'd done it or if she did, but we found ourselves in her opulent flat in Knightsbridge. I didn't see it. I didn't need to.

I didn't need anything but my Angel and her breaths on my lips, her moans in my ear, her warm body in my hands.

And then I didn't see anything at all but the backs of my eyelids as her tongue stroked the pulse point on my neck as she clawed at my sodden sweater.

My fingers tugged at the blouse that refused to lose its purchase on her skin, and it pissed me off enough that instead of the delicacy I planned to take with her, I ripped the fabric away from her skin without meaning to.

"Shit, babe. I didn't mean to rip it," I murmured my apology but by her giggle, she didn't care.

Then she returned the favor by ruining my shirt as well as she ran a long black talon down the center of my sweater, parting the wool from my flesh. I couldn't say why that caused such an intense curl of heat in my gut, but I wanted her more than I ever had at that second.

It isn't until her whole body freezes do I snap out of my lust-filled trance.

"What?" I asked cupping her jaw in my palm and tipping her chin so her eyes met mine.

"Your tattoo," she whispered.

"Which one, babe? There isn't much skin that isn't tattooed."

One cool finger traced the large calligraphy 'E' over my heart, and I froze. I'd gotten it one rare night off in the fifties. The green cast to the ink a dead giveaway of the age of the tattoo.

"It's old," she murmured.

"It is," I admitted, but she didn't need to know just how old it was.

She took my non-answer in stride, nodding as if she knew the whole story when I gave her only bits and pieces. I vowed there and then to give her more even if I couldn't give her all of me.

I backed up until my legs hit the soft cushion of her couch, and then I sat with my beautiful prize in my lap, moving my hands from her hips to cup her face, I brought her face to mine. Brushed my lips across her cheekbone, down the delicate column of her neck, nipped at her collarbone, tore the remnants of her shirt away to run my fangs over the crown of her shoulder. That one earned me a shiver so fierce she practically vibrated in my hands, her mewling moans causing my dick to jerk behind my zipper. I ran my nose back up her neck, memorizing the delicate scent of her and wondering if her pussy smelled the same.

My mouth watered, my cock pulsed, and I froze for a moment to collect myself before I lost all reason. Impatient, she quit waiting for me to undress her and reached behind her back to unclasp her bra. When the magenta lace fell away to reveal her creamy swells, my brain quit functioning except for my baser instincts.

My only thought was her scent, her sounds and the pale flesh beneath my rough fingertips.

I stood without preamble and headed for the dark hallway that I hoped held her bedroom. I hit pay dirt on the last room and laid her down on her king size bed. Shifting her to the center of the bed, I luckily had the forethought to drag her jeans and panties down her legs. My brain pressed pause on the moment—freezing it in my mind so I never, ever forgot the slim line of her legs, the dainty patch of blond curls at her center, her hips, her high, firm breasts, her neck, her face, her wild hair splayed all over her pillow. Her cheeks rosy from arousal and her eyes shining bright yet heavy lidded with want.

How did I get so lucky?

"If you don't take off those pants and get up here, I'm going to lose my, West," she grumbled, snapping me out of my reverie. I ripped my boots off my feet and shoved my jeans down my thighs and off, before climbing onto the bed between her legs.

She reached for my face, bringing her mouth to mine and I was done. Decades of wanting, decades of needed her, and now I had my Angel. I ran my blunt fingers through her wet heat, testing her readiness before notching my dick against her, feeling her slick arousal. At her needy moan, I pressed forward, her flesh parting around me, her gasps hitting me straight in my gut.

Hot, wet, tight.

I couldn't think of anything but her sounds—the gasping groans mixed with almost agonized whimpers of need, the smell of her neck, the feel of her desperate pants against my neck as I move in and out of her. And when her whole body tightened like the string of a bow —her arms closing around my shoulders, her legs becoming vices on my hips, her heat tightening on my cock—I lost it.

My fangs descended, the phase taking over before I have a chance to stop it. I had to fight every instinct I have not to rip into the meat of her shoulder as she breaks. Her moans reached my ears, and I was lost, pounding into her until my release came over me, groaning into the skin of her chest through gritted teeth.

Lifting my head, I looked at her smiling mouth, unable to stop the kisses I rained down on her face and neck. And when her lips caught mine I reveled in her warmth. When the kiss ended, her smile was all I needed, and it was easy to coax her to consume again— to live again.

We were happy.

For a time.

WEST—1995—OUTER BANKS, NC

We were sleeping naked and wrapped around each other when I nearly lost her.

It's funny how little we thought of the outside world

—how little we thought of the consequences of my life before her. But physics has it right. For every action, there is an equal and opposite reaction.

Even if it's a hundred some odd years late.

I was dreaming—dreaming of her running away from me and me chasing her, a game we used to play. Evangeline loved cat and mouse. She would pop in my workshop, poke me in the belly, say 'You're it!' and pop back out, practically begging for me to chase her— usually when I'd been working on an engine too long. I loved the game and her, mostly because she got me out of my own head. She got me to have fun. She got me to forget. The game usually ended with us wrapped around each other in bed—just like we were right then.

But this dream was so much different than all the others. It didn't feel playful, it felt like she was running from someone or thing. In my dream, she looked frightened, so when I shook myself out of it, I was already on high alert. Had I woken up a second later, we both would have died.

I saw a glint of moonlight coming in through the open French doors, reflecting off the steel of a rather large hunting knife.

Just one second later and her light would be out, and that one second would haunt me for the rest of my life. I didn't wait, I tightened my hold on her still-sleeping form and traveled to the panic room I set up in an interior, windowless room on the bottom floor.

By then, she was awake, and I threw clothes at her as I tried to dress, grab weapons from their assigned pegs and get back to the men who broke into our island house with not so much as a whisper.

"West, wait," she said as she grabbed my elbow, but I couldn't look at her.

I couldn't—I was too guilty.

I left her there in that steel-walled room, and even after I eliminated the threat—a family member of a target I'd ended at John's insistence when he'd murdered four small children—it was a long time before I spoke again.

WEST—A FEW MONTHS AGO—GRAND LAKE, CO

We were in the loft of the lake house, and I'd about had it with this woman. We'd just left Aurelia and Rhys to find the exceedingly romantic room Evangeline decorated. She'd said she was done with these two *'dancing around each other.'*

"You just can't let it go, can you?" she griped after I'd asked her for the tenth time.

"I know you're going somewhere without me—

which in this particular climate is not only scary, it is dumb as shit. Now, where is it?" I demanded.

She was. I'd lose her for hours where she wasn't with Aurelia, and she wasn't home or at the gallery. Where in the blue fuck was she?

"I was with Mom, okay? She's dying, West. The both of them are. Where else would I be?"

"Was that so damn hard? It's my job to keep you safe, but you keep secrets. You're even keeping secrets from Aurelia, and she's your best friend. I've been your Guardian for over a century, and she didn't know who I was until an hour ago. What the fuck, Evangeline? You ashamed of me or something?"

"Shouldn't I ask you that question?"

"You know why I won't. Outer Banks proved it, so don't tell me I'm a paranoid asshole. Look at your mom and dad. Look at them, and tell me you want to watch me die just so you can follow."

I regretted the last sentence as soon as it passed my lips, but the expression on her face was the worst sort of punishment. She looked like I'd just slapped her, and the tears welling in her eyes broke me.

"Dammit," I muttered as I crossed the loft, crowding her space, and cupping her small, delicate face in my rough hands. Her skin was like silk, and it had been so long since I'd felt it against my fingertips.

"I love you. I've always loved you. Do not punish me for wanting to keep you safe, Angel," I said before I ran my lips over her closed, wet eyelids, over the bridge of her nose, over her parted lips.

I stopped there, tasting her, feeling the heat of her that we'd denied ourselves for so long.

"Just don't leave me again," she ordered.

"I swear, Angel. If you want me to go, you're going to have to send me away."

"I'll hold you to that," I said, and if everything had gone to plan, she would have been my mate that night.

But when in my life had things ever gone to plan?

That's right. Never.

14

EVAN

Time stood still as I watch my friends—my family—try to breathe life into the man I couldn't live without. It was then that I completely understood why the Fates decided to make mates. Because if you loved someone just that much, when they left this world, you'd want to follow them.

There were so many regrets I had when it came to West, but the single largest thing I regretted was the time we wasted. The time I spent mad at him for doing what he believed in. The time we spent apart.

I was torn. Did I stay and watch Mena and Ian try to put him together? Or did I scour this most likely empty house for the person who hurt him?

So much death. So much pain.

No one should have to endure this, but especially not him. Not my West. It isn't fair or right that he should have to bear so much.

I don't lose it until Ian starts the chest compressions, climbing up on the rack to get the right angle. Until I hear his poor ribs crack with the force of them. Until Mena tells him to move so she can try to restart his heart. All the while, unbreakable arms hold me back as I try to get to him. Clawing, biting, kicking, I can't break them.

In my haze of anger and fear and regret, I barely notice the man hovering just out of the shadows, but when I catch a glimpse of white-blond hair, fury floods me. My power leaks from my skin—enough that the four men holding me so Ian and Mena can work unheeded, go flying outward like rag dolls.

My bonds gone, I stalk across the circular chamber to the place where I saw him, but nothing remains. No clue, nothing to prove the flash of blond was anything other than my imagination conjuring up something to keep my mind busy while I wait to know if the man I love is alive or dead. At first, I thought it was Walter, but the more I think about it, the more I'm sure it wasn't. And I know my mind must be playing tricks on me.

Why else would I see a man who died over a

hundred years ago? I watched Devereux Emerson die with my own eyes in 1906.

Didn't I?

"He's breathing!" Mena yells, and I forget the man who was never there in the first place and go to West.

"He's still unconscious, and we need to get to a medical facility right now, but he's alive," Ian informs me, but I can't think about that right now.

All I can do is play *'he's alive'* in my head over and over again.

"You have what you need at the high-rise or do we need to commandeer a surgical suite at the local hospital?" I ask him. Ian has been outfitting the new headquarters into a better facility than we had in Grand Lake, but getting all the things we need takes time.

"I'm going to need the hospital," Ian replies, "And we need to be quick about it. He has some internal bleeding—I'm sure of it."

"I have a contact at the local university hospital. She was going... to help me leave before I got caught trying to get the ch-children out," Claire struggles to say behind us. "I-I could call her if someone has a phone. There are good people there. It is a safe place."

Carver passes over his cell, and he and Claire travel from the chamber to find a place that actually has cell service.

"I don't even know if he should travel," Mena mutters under her breath. "I'm not sure he'd survive the trip. We need a car or an ambulance or something. He's... drawing on me still. I can't let him go or..." She shakes her head.

"We'll do small distances," Asher offers. "There is no way we can make it up those stairs carrying him. I say we take him to the foyer first."

"I can carry West and Mena, but I need you to follow close," I tell Asher and Ian. Turning to Aidan and Cam, "I need you to find a car and get it to the front door. Now."

Carver and Claire pop back in the room. "My friend is setting up the OR now," she informs us.

"How long is the drive?" Ian asks.

"About twenty minutes. Ten if we hurry," Claire says.

"Let's go," I order and smoke out with my hands on Mena and West from this horrible room to the foyer then to the back of the SUV that screeches up to the front door. It's a tight fit, but since all the seats are laid down in the back, we can squeeze in.

"Meet us there," Mena yells through the glass to Asher, Carver and Claire as we speed off through the night hoping we make it in time.

I brush West's long, blood-crusted hair away from

his face. If I didn't know him, if I didn't love him, I would never recognize him. His eyes are swollen shut, his nose mangled, his full lower lip split clean through. I don't realize I'm trembling until I see my shaking hand hover over his injuries. I don't know where to touch him so it won't hurt. I don't know what I'm supposed to do.

Doing the only thing I can, I brush his hair back and kiss him on the only uninjured part of his whole body. I press my lips to his forehead and pray with everything in me he stays alive.

It doesn't take us twenty or even ten minutes to get to the hospital.

It takes us eight.

Nurses are waiting for us with a gurney when we screech up to the emergency room entrance, and they help us carefully extract West's limp body from the back of the SUV. I have to give it to Claire, she was right—this is a safe place. The four nurses that met us are made up of a Phoenix, two Witches and some sort of Shifter. I follow them as they haul ass into the hospital through the emergency room entrance straight to an OR elevator. When I try to follow, two sets of hands hold me back.

"Let them work, darling girl," Aurelia says in my ear when I struggle against Cam and Aidan's hold. I turn, spying my best friend. She's here right when I need her, and I can't help but break. I slam into her with a hug so tight it's possible I cracked a rib.

"When did you get here? How?" I question muffled by tears as I burrow my face in the leather of her jacket.

"Voyt and Kyle brought us when Carver gave me a call about the hospital," she says. "He thought you might need me."

"He's... he's *hurt,* Ari. Do you... do you know if..."

I can't even finish that sentence. I don't think I want to know if he's leaving me yet.

"I don't know what's going to happen, baby girl. All we can do it wait," she says as she squeezes me tight.

EIGHT HOURS.

We waited eight hours in a private operating room lobby on the stiff vinyl benches, picking over fast food remnants and vending machine offerings.

Waiting for word, for hope. Waiting for West.

Well, waiting and trying to calm Kyle down when he found out we didn't find Nicola along with West. It took some doing, but we convinced him we would work together to find her, and while he wasn't appeased, he took one look at my pleading face and sat the fuck down.

The surgeon who emerges from the automatic double doors has carefully masked her features. Why do doctors do that? Any facial expression at all would be better than this.

"Mrs. Carmichael?" she says as she scans the room for me. The name gives me pause, but whatever she needs to call me to give me what I want to know is good with me. It doesn't matter how many times I'd wished for someone to call me by that name, and if it is the last time someone does it, at least I got it once.

"Th-that's me," I croak, struggling to stand under the weight of the unknown.

Aurelia grabs my hand and we stand together. The smile that breaks across her face nearly makes my legs give out in relief.

"He's alive, ma'am, and doing well. There was a severe bleed in his abdomen, and we had to remove his spleen, but we got it under control. We're going to need to watch him for a few days, but given his species, he should make a full recovery. This hospital is a safe zone, so whomever did this cannot enter. It is appropriately warded against it."

"Good," I sob in relief. "Can I see him?"

"Absolutely. Follow me," she says as she leads me to a private recovery room where I see the best thing ever.

West. Safe and warm and alive.

Wasting no time, I rush to his side. His face is still mangled, but his nose has been set and he's breathing on his own, so I don't give one single shit if he has scars or if he's disfigured. He's alive and mine, and if I had half a mind and he were anywhere near able, I'd bite him and cement the bond. Screw this *the man has to bond the woman'* bullshit.

Damn patriarchal society. Always screwing shit up.

Climbing as carefully as I can into the bed beside him, I curl like a cat into his side and settle in to wait some more.

I can wait forever if he's breathing beside me.

EVAN—1991—SORRENTO, ITALY

We lounged on beach chairs on the black sands of a little inlet in the cliff face. The turquoise water lapped calmly against the beach, and I was finally at peace. One better, West was right beside me, sunning himself. His wide, muscular body exposed to the warm rays of a beautiful Italian summer.

His tattoos were on display for all the world to see, but the one that meant the most to me was the large stylized 'E' tattooed right over his heart. He'd had it long before we got together. I saw it the first time we made love on that cold winter night in England four years ago. I knew right away what it was and what it meant. The ink slightly faded with age, the greenish cast that most older tattoos had, I knew then he'd loved me for much longer than he'd let on. I didn't need any more than that.

He still refused to cement the bond, but I'd wait. I'd wait forever for him.

"You want to go swimming, Angel?" he asked turning to his side to watch me, his voice a quiet rumble in the calm.

"No, babe," I said shaking my head. "I just want to doze. Wake me if I start to burn?"

"Sure, darlin'."

"Love you," I said as I drifted off into a light doze.

So I heard him when he said, "Love you, too, Angel. Love you, too."

And because I heard the gruff timber of his voice, I knew I was safe, and I had sweet dreams.

15

WEST

I can't decide if I'm in Heaven or Hell. I'm warm for the first time in a month, so that's a plus. The fact that my entire body feels like it has been run over twice by a semi-truck is definitely going in the minus column. But the best feeling—the absolute best thing in this world or the next—filters through my consciousness despite the pain.

The warmth and softness of my Angel pressing against my side.

I feel the pull of my answering smile yank at the stitches in my lip, and it all comes filtering back.

The dungeon. Nicola. Emerson... he put a soul in her. A soul summoned from the depths of the worst pit of

Hell. I have no idea how he did it or how he knew how to do it. And I have the worst feeling I know exactly who he put in her.

But why? What does he have to gain by putting the woman who damn near exterminated us back into this world?

Evangeline. He wants to kill Evangeline.

My eyes jerk open to reveal the off-white acoustic tiles of a hospital ceiling, and I frown, confused. Hospital? If I'm in a hospital, it must be really bad. I have half a mind to lift the sheet to make sure I still have all my bits and pieces, but I'm having the hardest time moving my arms.

I have to tell her. I have to tell her what they did...

Instead, the pull of sleep—something I'd been missing out on considerably over the last month—yanks at my consciousness, and I succumb to the darkness with my Angel at my side.

I wake again to the sun filtering through the blinds of my hospital room and Evangeline snoring next to me. I always found it hilarious that someone so small was capable of sounding like a freight train when she's really out of it. It's how I know she hasn't been sleeping, she hasn't been taking care of herself. She only snores when she is truly exhausted.

I look down at the mess of curls spilling over my

shoulder and bare chest. Her eyes have deep purple shadows underneath them, and the arm gently wrapped around my chest is one step away from skeletal.

How did they let her get this bad? How did they let her go that long without eating? Without consuming?

This is my fault.

I should have made the time to bind her. I should have put away my own bullshit and took care of her. She was losing her parents, and I was stuck in my own head so much I didn't see what I was doing wasn't what she needed. What I was doing was pushing her away.

But it doesn't matter what happened in the past— the fights and disagreements and all the other bullshit. I have her, and that is all that matters now.

She makes a highly indelicate and downright hilarious snort in her sleep, and I can't help but laugh. I regret it instantly. Red hot fire runs through my chest and gut.

Holy shit, that hurts.

Evangeline rouses from her sound sleep at my pained groan.

"West? Baby?" she calls to me, wide awake. "Are you okay? Do I need to call a doctor?"

I shake my head, but just then, the door opens, and Aurelia drags Mena by the hand into the room. Mena's eyes flash, and she reaches for my shoulder placing her healing hand on my skin. The relief I feel is immediate, but it doesn't cure everything. Rhys and Asher file in next.

"Well, that sucked," I groan.

"Yeah, yesterday pretty much sucked all around. Good to have you awake, man," Rhys murmurs, subdued.

"Okay? What did I miss? Why does everyone look like somebody died?"

"Four children were found in the dungeon where you were held," Mena informs me, the only one of the women in the room whose eyes aren't swimming in tears.

"What? Are they okay?" I ask aloud, but even I know it is probably the dumbest question I could ask.

If they were okay—these children—Aurelia wouldn't be shaking her head at me as tears pour down her face. Evangeline wouldn't be holding in her sobs by the skin of her teeth. Mena wouldn't be looking at me with dead eyes. And Rhys and Asher wouldn't be staring at me like they're just glad I'm alive.

I didn't know there were children down there with us, and now all I'd gone through seems trivial, selfish even. Because I made it out. I'm alive. I've lived longer than I ever thought possible, and these kids barely lived at all. Brutality towards children kills me. It brings up so many old ghosts. Ghosts of a long dead father who was the vilest man I'd known of until this moment.

"Do we…" I choke out. "Do we know who the children are? Have we informed their parents?"

"We've called in the faction representatives," Mena answers. "We're doing the hard shit here where it is neutral. This hospital is warded against malevolent activity. Harm can't be done on the grounds. They'll be here soon," Asher says.

"I want to go with you. To tell the families."

"I don't think that's a good idea," Aurelia mutters.

"I don't either," Evan says.

"Those families are going to come here, sit down in a conference room or waiting area or whatever and get the worst news they've ever received. Someone who was there with their children needs to be there when you tell them."

"And what happens when they see your broken but breathing self in that room, and they decide you need to die, too? Huh?" Evan demands. "You can't stay in this hospital forever."

"I think I have given up too much of my life worrying that someone will come after me for the things I've done or the things I couldn't control. If they have that much hate in their hearts for someone who barely made it out, then let them come. But I don't think we need to discount them just yet."

My Angel's answering growl tells me I've won this argument. She hops off the bed and slams out of the room. She returns a few moments later with a wheel-chair and Ian, who goes to my left arm and the IV in my hand. He deftly removes it, turns off machines, and shoos everyone out of the room before he helps with the transfer from the bed to the chair.

It sucks that he had to do it, but there is no way in hell I'd make it on my own. Sitting up took pretty much everything I had even with the handy dandy motorized bed helping me out with eighty percent of it. I'm just lucky I'm dressed from the waist down. Ian passes me a scrub top which matches the blue bottoms, and I struggle to get it over my head.

Two small hands help me tug the fabric down the rest of the way over my eyes, and my Angel is there.

I grab one of her delicately fragile hands and turn it over so I can kiss the center of her palm. I move it to the center of my chest, and I say the words I've needed to say since the beginning.

"I'm staying with you, and you're staying with me. I'm not letting you do the hard shit alone anymore. Don't be mad at me for not wanting to abandon you again. Okay?" I murmur, and I watch as her expression goes from pissed to tearful in an instant.

"Do you promise?" she asks.

"I swear," I whisper as I reach up to cup her jaw in my hands and bring her down to me. "I'm never leaving you again, Evangeline. Even if you send me away."

She laughs through a sob at my pronouncement.

"I really wish I could kiss you right now," she grumbles.

"I do, too, Angel," I murmur as I rest her forehead on mine for a moment before she gently kisses the tip of my nose and moves to the back of the chair.

"Let's go do the hard shit," she says as we walk through the door into the hallway and toward another form of Hell.

The room they put us in to break the news is larger than I expected. It has couches and comfy chairs, and even though someone was kind enough to bring platters full of Danish and croissants splayed on the large sideboard at the back of the room, I can't bring myself to eat. It doesn't matter that I can't remember when the last time I ate was.

What matters is Evangeline and Mena have to tell these faction leaders that their young ones have died, and it was at Wraith hands. Here's hoping it doesn't start a war.

Two men and a woman file into the room. The first man is medium height, maybe just under six feet and built with dark hair and pale amber eyes that flash like a cat's in the florescent light. *The Shifter representative.* He's dressed casually in a flannel shirt and jeans, and I expect if he weren't frowning in preparation for the news he's about to receive, he'd be smiling. Laugh lines radiate from his eyes, and he has a peace about him I wish I had.

The second man is abnormally tall, so much so he has to duck considerably at the threshold to get in the room. He's painfully thin, and his thinness is high-lighted by the black suit hanging on his frame. *Warlock.* His face is impassive, if a little worried.

The woman is nothing how I would expect a Witch to dress—she's buttoned up to her neck in a black on black pantsuit and heels. She too is gaunt, and her ash blonde hair is pulled back so severely from her face, I half expect to see blood at her scalp. Her face is what gives me pause. If there were one I'd bet on giving us some trouble, it'd be her. Most Witches are neutral, but this one has evil tattooed on her face in the form of a sneer. Plus, she smells like a damn snack, so I know she's the damn devil.

Phoenixes and Wraiths don't hang out much with other factions, but if we did, we'd have the upper hand in most situations because we can smell a double-dealing psychopath a mile away. And this bitch smells like Sunday dinner.

Greetings are said, hands are shook, but when they sit in their seats, I can tell they have a good idea what they're doing here.

The first man, the Shifter, Anthony, pipes up.

"Well, out with it. I have fifteen missing children in my community, I'm assuming you found them?"

Evangeline's face goes gray. "Fif-fifteen?" she asks before shaking her head. "We recovered the bodies of four children in our raid on Walter Emerson's house. Two shifter children, one Warlock, and one Witch. We did not find anyone else in the house except for Claire and West, and had we taken any longer to find him, he would have been among the dead. Claire was caught trying to free the children, and either because he was her father or he just wanted her to die slowly, he left her beaten in a cell with no food, water, or way out. As far as we know, no one else was in the house," she says squeezing my hand tight so her voice doesn't falter again.

I have never been more proud of her than I am right now, and even though I wish I could take this burden from her and shoulder it myself, I won't. She's doing what she needs to do to lead. Even the hard shit. *Espe-cially* the hard shit.

"We didn't send them on yet. We wanted to inform you of their passing so you could help their families put them to rest. We will be more than willing to help you with the funeral rites if you so choose," Mena informs them.

Anthony and the Warlock, Sebastian look stunned, but the Witch, Tessa, does not. Her face doesn't change at all.

"You only found two?" Anthony asks.

"Yes, but are you sure there are fifteen that you are missing? Do you... do you mind if I touch you? I'd see better if I did," Aurelia says from her chair. "I might be able to see if they've passed."

Anthony nods and Aurelia places her hand on his exposed forearm. Her eyes immediately light up with a vision, but by her tears the news is the worst kind. Her eyes dim and when they can focus again, she looks at the three faction leaders.

Her face ravaged, she says, "I know where your missing children are."

"Where are they, child?" Sebastian asks. It is the first time he's spoken, and I had no idea his voice would be as kind as it is.

"They're buried in the woods."

16

EVAN

I never wanted to come back to this house. I didn't want West here either. Especially him. I don't know the extent of the hell he lived through as a child, but I know there was abuse. He doesn't have to tell me for me to know there were horrendous things done to him. And bringing him back to this place makes me sick to my stomach.

Mena and Aurelia won't step a single toe on the Oregon property where they were tortured, and if Aurelia had her way, they'd burn it to the ground. So to have West, Voyt, and Kyle here when they so recently endured so much pain, makes me angry, it makes my heart hurt, makes me hate my own kind.

And Claire...

West told me he could tell right away she'd been abused—before he even learned her name, he knew. I hate that he can recognize it so easily in another victim. I cannot fathom the atrocities she's been subjected to, and I can't stand this for them.

But there are children out there that need to be put to rest, and we have a murderer—or murderers—to find. I'd thought I had started to make a difference for my people, but letting Walter run free will haunt me to the day I die.

We're sitting in the SUV we commandeered from Walter's garage, and I'm having the hardest time making myself let go of West's hand so I can step out and deal with the horrors committed here. I want to tell Rhys to just drive on, but Aurelia takes the decision out of my hands as she opens the door and shakily steps down from the front passenger seat. Rhys is with her in a flash, holding her up as she walks on trembling legs not in the direction of the house, but to the trees.

I go to open my door when West squeezes my hand to stop me.

"I want you to stop worrying about me, Angel. I'm alive, and I'll heal. You need to worry about what happened here and watch your back around the Witch. You don't need to worry about anything else. Okay?"

I nod, but the thought that has been running on loop in my head spills out of my mouth.

"Is this my fault? Did changing everything about our community make him do this? Did I cause this?" West pulls my hand and then I'm in his arms, wrapped in his warmth, his strength.

"No, babe. He caused this. He did what he did and was doing it for a long time. Anthony said they've been searching for these kids for months. Not weeks. Months. Walter has been doing this for a while, and nothing you did was going to change it."

"Then why do I feel like it is? Why do I feel like I could have prevented this?"

He shakes his head at me and presses a kiss to my forehead.

"Because you give a shit, Angel," he murmurs into my hair. "But you cannot predict or control the actions of evil men any more than you can change the stars in the sky. So why would you take the blame for them?"

I shrug, giving him a slight squeeze before turning and exiting the SUV. In an instant, Cam and Aidan are at my side.

"We would like to be within arm's reach of you the entire time you are on this property, Evan. It is imperative you stay with us," Aidan says in my ear before I can take another step.

"Please," Cam throws in.

"The Witch?" I ask.

"Someone had to ward the place, and one that big, it had to be a powerful Witch who did it. Plus, she smells... *tasty*. Keep your weapons on you and stay close. I don't know what kind of juju she has under her belt, but I don't want to take any chances," Cam confirms.

I nod and open my emerald cashmere knee-length coat that Aurelia so graciously brought with her, to show Aidan and Cam the under arm holster holding my Glock and the tri-dagger sheathed at the hip of my leather fighting pants.

"I'm good. But if I'm moving, you need to stay with me. Got it?" I order. I have a feeling things are about to go to shit real quick."

"Aurelia rubbing off on you?" Aidan half jokes.

"Maybe."

We walk in the direction Aurelia headed in—the same place we fought so many Guardians—and I feel like an idiot for not seeing it earlier. At the edge of the forest, the ground is disturbed. Not enough that we would have seen it or distinguished it in the night when we raided, but enough that I feel like an imbecile now. The slight mounds of the shallow graves are in a tri-semicircle pattern similar to a Celtic knot, but the mounds are so small, they could easily be confused for varying elevation in the night.

How did we miss the feel of it, though? How did we miss the call of so many souls?

Anthony, Sebastian, and Tessa have followed close behind us, and we all stand in a loose circle around the disturbed earth.

"There are t-twenty ch-children here," Aurelia says, shivering while cradling her middle, protecting her unborn children as she witnesses Hell behind her glowing eyes. To anyone else, she looks like she'll be sick to her stomach—and she might—but I know what she's doing. This is a nightmare for me, but for someone who has already lost one child and is terrified of losing another, she is looking at her own personal version of Hell.

"Some-someone was using them. Stealing their power…" she says as she trails off and her eyes dim again. Rhys holds her up as she sags in his arms. When she can stand again, she doesn't look at anyone but Tessa. Her upper lip curls into a snarl, and she goes from sagging to phased in an instant—wings rip through the thick gray wool sweater as they burst from her back.

West was right—we needed to watch out for Tessa.

"How many did you kill personally? Ten? All twenty?" Aurelia asks Tessa, her eyes glowing white, flames licking up her arms as her wings spread wide. Rhys, spurred by his wife, phases immediately.

Tessa's eyes go wide as she starts to back away from my flaming best friend and her husband. She doesn't make it two steps before she runs into Mena and Asher. Both of them phase in an instant—Mena's blue flames and wings paired with the electricity pulsing like lightning across her skin and Asher's talons and fangs erupting in a swath of black smoke. Tessa edges away from them and runs into a fully phased Ian and Carver; then she runs into Claire. I never expected Claire to be anything even marginally resembling fierce, but phased and pissed off—she is more than terrifying.

Tessa flinches away from her and into Anthony and Sebastian. Anthony's eyes flash gold, and the rumbling growl ripping up his throat sounds similar to a cougar. Sebastian is the only one of us who is completely silent, but his once impassive face is now gone to reveal a look so deadly, if I were Tessa, I'd be terrified. Right now all I can feel is rage.

I sense more than see West's arrival at my back.

"Where is Walter, Tessa?" he growls the question I hadn't thought to ask. I hadn't thought anything past ripping her limb from limb with my talons. "Did you help him raise Iva?"

I'm glad he's asking questions. I'm glad he has his

head in the sea of bloodlust, but I would expect nothing less of him. Despite all his protests about worthiness, West is more equipped to be a King than I am to be a Queen.

"Why are you people trying to attack me? I have done nothing wrong!" she insists, her voice frantic, but her face betrays her. I see the cruel twist to her mouth and the cold deadness to her eyes. She doesn't care about the loss of life. She doesn't give one single shit about the lives she stole from these children or the agony their parents will feel or the light she snuffed out.

"Killing innocent children is wrong. Using the deaths of children for your own gain is wrong," his furious voice rumbles, livid that he has to explain this shit.

Aurelia, tired of Tessa's stalling, grabs her forearm with her burning hand and asks again.

"Where is Walter, Tessa?" Aurelia asks through gritted teeth, but all Tessa can do is scream.

Aurelia lets her go, and she drops into a ball of agony on the forest floor.

"I-I didn't k-kill them. I j-just did the s-spell," she sobs. "It was Devereux. He killed the children. F-for the spell. I needed the p-power," she confesses as she cradles her now blackened forearm.

"Devereux Emerson?" I ask, but I know. I could have

sworn I saw him in the chamber, but I'd just brushed it off to stress and my guilty mind.

But when she nods...

"He died in 1906. I watched a blade pierce his damn neck," I argue.

Tessa shakes her head. "If you think Iva is the first soul Walter Emerson forced me to bring back, you are sadly mistaken."

"No reason on this earth or the next absolves your hand in this, Tessa. You are complicit in these murders and just as responsible," Sebastian decrees. "You have upset the balance, and as such you. Will. Burn," he snarls as he gives Aurelia a nod.

Aurelia's lips curl back from her teeth in snarl as she grabs Tessa by her throat. Aurelia's fire burns hotter, brighter as she lifts Tessa off of her feet and into the air and coats her body in flames. Tessa's scream quickly trickles off to a gurgle and then to nothing. Her body crumbles to ash and bone, slipping through Aurelia's fingers.

"You need to deport her sorry ass to Hell, Evan," Aurelia practically orders me, and although I agree, I shouldn't be the one to do it. I can't be the one.

"West can. He needs it more," I tell her, but I feel the squeeze of West's fingers at my shoulder.

"You need this, Angel. I'll get the next one," he whispers in my ear.

"I'll lose it. There are too many souls. I'll take the wrong ones. I can't do this here with all of these people. I could hurt someone," I whisper back furiously.

He brings a finger to my chin and turns my head so I meet his eyes. His expression tells me he's digging in. He won't take the soul—even though he needs it. Even though he's hurt and barely healing and in pain.

Stalemate.

17

WEST

Evangeline has lost her mind if she thinks I'm taking this soul when she's so hungry. By her face, she's thinking the same damn thing about me. The stubborn twist to her mouth tells me I'm going to lose this one.

"I'm not going to argue with you about it. This is not the time nor the place to have this discussion. Take the damn soul, West. I will get the next one," she whispers furiously through gritted teeth.

Out of all of us, she is the only one in control.

She always is.

I love it and hate it all at the same time. But then, I see how close to losing it she is. How frightened she is that she will hurt someone. How much pain she's in so she doesn't mess up and take good souls to Hell. Her pale blue eyes beg me for understanding.

So, I concede, phasing as quickly as my battered body will allow, feeling the ache in my jaw as my fangs break free, the bitter sting in my fingertips as my talons grow despite the fact that they'd been ripped out during my torture. I unhinge my jaw the same way a snake would and breathe in the soul.

For so many years I hated what I was, hated that we as Wraiths had to consume so much evil just to survive. I assume my Angel hates herself just as much as I did at her age. I see it differently than I did as a younger man —we are keeping the balance. We are making the world safer and if that brings us nourishment, well then, so be it.

Tessa's soul gives me energy, heals some of the most superficial of my wounds, and eases the ache in my abdomen. But with the good, comes the bad. I can see every single stain on her soul and for a woman less than half my age, she had many. The children she's slaughtered at her own hand for power. The abilities she stole by way of torture. The Witches she shunned—cutting them off from their families so they had nothing and no one. The damned souls she brought back from Hell and the good souls she stole from the heavens at their parent's command.

Including Devereux Emerson.

I have no idea what to do about him or the fact that he and his brother's deaths were the reason Evangeline demolished an entire city. And if I have to venture a guess, he was the man who nearly took my damn life.

I have to tell her, but it can't be right now.

"We need to put these children to rest. Aurelia. Mena. Rhys. Help them identify their dead, and get the souls taken care of. A few of us are going to search the rest of the property. Claire, I need you to show us around the grounds," Evangeline orders, snapping us out of the feral bloodlust.

She's right. We do have a job to do.

Evangeline turns to go but immediately comes back to grab my hand before getting the fuck out of there, marching double time back to the cars. She's shaking, practically vibrating with the strain of holding back. I yank on her hand, pulling her into my arms as she breaks. Aidan, Cam, and Claire stand back for a moment as my Angel tries to get herself under control.

"Th-those children. All those lives. I couldn't do it. I couldn't consume her with them so close. I couldn't... What if I took them with her? What if I consumed too much and hurt people?" she sobs, her breathing picking up to full-blown panic attack hyperventilation.

"Shh, Angel," I murmur into her hair as I wrap her

up in my arms. "We'll get you consuming again. We'll start small, and it'll just be you and me."

Her head snaps up at that moment as her nostrils flare. Her eyes bleed from blue to black, her fangs snap down, talons erupting from her fingertips. I realize pretty quickly there is another soul out here. I didn't notice before, but now that I'm not in pain my mind is clearer and I can sense it.

But the Evangeline I know is not here right now. This woman before me is a feral representation of my Angel, and she's three steps past hungry.

She's famished, and there is something to eat, or rather some*one*.

She breaks from my hold, taking off into a sprint. Not for the house or the forest but for the water of the lake. Cam and Aidan rush after her, but I can feel it—the tasty morsel she's heading toward—so I travel there to wait for her because there is no chance in hell I'm running.

I make it to the wooden planking of the path to the boathouse before she does, but that doesn't stop her. Evangeline leaps into the air, plants both hands and feet on my chest, and takes me down to the ground as she uses my body like a fucking springboard to get past me. It would be hot as hell if she didn't just pop some of my staples and knock the breath out of me.

I turn and scramble to my feet, hobbling for a moment until Cam and Aidan come up behind me and grab me by the arms to chase her down.

Shit. Fuck. Motherfucking shit. Holy Fates that hurts.

We bust through the already obliterated boathouse door to see Evangeline stalking around Walter's body. By the looks of him, he's been dead about a day. The pooled blood around his still stiff body is nearly congealed, so I'm not worried that she killed him.

I'm more worried about her ability to discern reason at this point. Oh, and that whole *please -don't-eat-him* thought that seems to be running on a constant loop in my brain. I'm prepared to tackle her, and I'm honestly scared I might have to—popped staples or not.

She circles him like an animal on the hunt, her nostrils flaring. The crack of her jaw audibly unhinging sends a shiver of unease down my spine. I don't know what I would do if she turned Revenant.

"Angel," I rasp, and her eyes snap to mine—clearing for a moment before falling back to her meal.

Her eyes fall closed, and she breathes him in, consuming him and transporting his vile soul to Hell. Immediately, her cheeks fill out, her color coming back. Such a change isn't normal. It had to have been months since her last feed. Fates. She had to be starving.

Evangeline phases back instantly, and her eyes

won't meet mine or Aidan's or Cam's. No. She's looking for the exit just behind us. Deciding it isn't worth the footwork, she travels from the room. My mind grays out for a second, and it is then I remember I popped staples in my gut. Looking down, I see my white shirt stained red.

Shit. If I faint, I'll never forgive myself.

I suck it up, hobbling out of the boathouse—away from Walter's ashes and the lingering stench of his corpse—and look for my Angel. It doesn't take too long to find her. She's busy puking her guts up on the grass at the lake's edge.

I make it over to her and plop to my ass, careful not to fall in the water, but just barely.

"Doing okay, Angel," I whisper as I start fading, holding onto my consciousness by a very thin thread.

She wipes her mouth, and brings her tear-filled eyes to mine.

"He hurt you. He hurt Claire. He hurt Devereux and Sam, and so many others. He did things I never want to say out loud. And I could have spared you so much pain if I would have just killed him when I had the chance. My father should have killed him. Someone should have stopped him and no one did. I hate feeling thankful to whomever took his life, but I am."

"You consumed and didn't lose it at least. Can we be happy about that?"

"Sure, I'll get right on that after we send murdered children off to their rest, hunt down a resurrected Guardian, and oh yeah, find the evil bitch they brought back from Hell because she wants to kill me before I kill her. I'll be sure to pencil in my happy time after that, mm-kay? There is no bright side situation in this scenario," she fires back.

"And I popped your staples. Fuck. Cam, can you see if Mena or Ian can do a patch job?" she asks him and he nods before traveling across the property rather than taking the hike.

Aidan looks down at me, and reaches in his back pocket for the clean handkerchief he keeps there, placing it on my open wound.

This day just sucks all around.

MENA WAS ABLE TO PATCH ME UP A BIT, AND IAN FIXED ME UP the rest of the way after they identified and put twenty souls to rest.

Evangeline was right. There was no bright side.

Doing everything they could think of, Aurelia and

Mena still couldn't find Nicola or Devereux. Anthony and Sebastian promised to put out every feeler and call in every favor to help find them, and since Claire had no clue her brother was even alive, so she was no help. I'm not sure how much I believe that, but Claire had been through enough without us badgering her. She didn't need more.

Devereux needs to be taken down—that wasn't the question, but Nicola... Her situation was sticky at best and fucking lethal at worst. The horrible question in everyone's mind was what to do when we found her. We didn't know what happened for certain, and without the knowing, there wasn't much we could do.

Kyle left us as soon as he was able. Evangeline didn't want him to go, but she couldn't blame him for wanting to search for his mate.

We all just hoped he didn't regret what he found.

18

I FEEL LIKE I HAVE BEEN WAITING FOR ONE THING OR ANOTHER my whole life. But most of my time has been waiting for West to get his head out of his ass.

Unfortunately, I'm still waiting.

It's been a week—a whole week—and I haven't gotten more than a one-word answer or a grunt in response to any question I've asked. He's lucky he's finally healed up, or I'd pop another staple just to get a reaction from him.

I know why he's pissed.

Well, I should say I know his reason, but not why. Who gives a shit if I saw what Walter did to him? I mean, it isn't like I didn't discover him in that damn chamber. It isn't like I didn't have his blood all over me as I prayed to the Fates not to take him too.

It's not like I didn't see.

But I did. I saw every cut and strike and slice. I saw everything he went through at Walter's hands. I saw what he made Devereux do to him too. Every bad thing, every murder, every single time he beat his children, every time he raped his wife, every underhanded deal and every soul he deported to Hell without reason or cause.

And people wonder why I don't consume. Because I don't want to see this shit.

But now he's all kinds of butt hurt about what I saw.

Does this make him feel vulnerable? Does he think I think less of him? Who fucking knows what is going on in his head. It's not me; that's for sure. It pisses me off to have him so close when he feels miles away.

I feel alone. Again. Even after he said he wouldn't leave, he's done it all the same.

I'm sitting at the dining room table in the high rise condo I purchased a month ago, picking at an omelet Cam shoved in front of me. I couldn't go back to the cliff house where my parents died, and I couldn't even pretend I wanted to go back to Grand Lake. It felt wrong there without them, and I couldn't bring myself to stay there when every wall held my mother's laughter and every single room was missing my father's presence.

Aidan and Cam have made it their mission to make sure I eat and consume. I'd venture a guess this is West's doing, but I can't be sure. Either way, the two of them have taken their Guardian duties to new levels.

Cam scrapes a dining chair back over the slate tiles, eliciting a lovely nails-on-a-chalkboard screech from the wrought iron legs on the stone. Sweet mother, I need a rug underneath this table.

"You going to eat or what?" Cam grumbles.

Appropriately scolded, I use my fork to slice into the fluffy concoction of eggs, bacon, red onion and green bell pepper. It smells wonderful and tastes even better. Who knew Cam could cook?

I inhale the eggs, and I realize I was more than hungry. Especially when I start looking around for more food. Cam rolls his eyes before getting up to warm up a whole slew of leftovers. Creamy sausage-potato-kale soup from Aurelia with crusty French bread, beef medallions topped with seared scallops, roasted asparagus and a mushroom risotto that makes my eyes roll back in my head. I eat enough for four people, and I'm not sorry.

After I finish my buffet of awesomeness, I shuffle off to my bed. I stop by my bathroom to do the whole face washing, teeth brushing, pajama donning deal and flop onto my bed with the last vestiges of my strength, promptly passing out.

Full bellies must be equivalent to tranquilizer darts, is my last thought before I'm dead to the world.

I wake up on my left side and warm for the first time in a week—since the last time I was in West's arms. He's in the bed with me, his delicious heat at my back, his breath and the whiskers of his beard tickling the sensitive skin of my neck. All week he's been sleeping in one of the eight guest rooms in the two-floor penthouse.

But this morning is different.

I am warm and content and so happy to have him next to me that it is a brutal slap to have reality seep into my brain. He's practically ignored me for a week— as if I did something wrong, as if I'm to blame somehow —and it pisses me off. So, despite the warmth, and strength of his massive arm curled around my body and the rough possessive hand he has inside my camisole over my left breast... and the thumb he has rolling over my nipple... and the hard, thick, naked cock against my backside... *mmm...*

Maybe I'm not as mad as I was before. I could totally give him the benefit of the doubt here. Give him a pass just this once.

I roll my hips against him, and the growl I get back sends a shiver down my spine. Okay, I'll be mad at him later. Tomorrow maybe, if he keeps playing with my nipple like that. His fangs graze the skin of my neck, and I freeze.

In all the time we have been together, West has never phased while we were making love. He has always held himself back, always in control. Always.

Because he never wanted me to hope. He never wanted to take the chance of losing control. This is huge. This is the equivalent of a man getting on one knee and showing a woman the rock. My heart swells so big, I want to cry. I'm holding on by a very thin thread as I turn in his arms to look at him.

"You sure? You can't take this back," I whisper, my voice trembling.

This—him—is what I've wanted since the beginning, but I'm torn between pissed off that he dragged his feet, taking his sweet ass time to get here, and so blindingly happy that I'm practically vibrating in his arms.

His gaze bores into me—reaches to the very depths of my soul. I don't need to ask again, and I don't need an answer. His face is his reply, and I feel it like a caress against my skin. His eyes bleed from black back to jade, his fangs retracting back into his jaw and he takes that moment to run lips across my forehead, the softness of lips followed by the gentle scratch of his beard over my cheekbones and down my neck. His hands make quick work of my camisole and sleep shorts, but he doesn't move to do anything else. He just holds my naked body against his, burying his head against my chest as he wraps me up in his arms. I sift my fingers through his shoulder-length hair, missing this closeness we had so long ago.

But the heat of his skin makes me restless, and the throbbing ache between my legs has me shifting and squirming in his arms. My body flashes hot all over and it is as if my blood is answering his call. The quick, hot lash of his tongue on my nipple pulls a moan from me and a growl from him which only gets louder once he pulls my nipple into his mouth and starts torturing me with his blunted teeth.

He rolls us, so I'm on my back with his massive body in between my legs. His lips are on mine then, and his kiss is a promise, a vow. He won't leave me. He won't abandon me. And if one of us leaves this earth, the other will be following close behind. His fingers tangle in my hair, and he gives a soft tug to get my attention. He has it, he so has it.

"I love you, Evangeline. Will you be mine?" his gruff, raspy voice asks.

I've been waiting for those words for a century. I've been waiting so long for them, I can't even speak. I can't do anything but nod, happy tears spilling from the corners of my eyes as I watch his emotions pass like an open book across his face. I see his love, his trust in his expression and I can't fathom how I could have thought he didn't. Then, his lips are on mine again, his tongue sliding into my mouth, and I want him so much. I want him inside of me. I want my blood inside his mouth, my essence in his heart. I want it all.

He gives me everything I want—everything I need —but he makes me wait, he makes me beg. His lips trail down my body, little nips and sucking kisses at my breasts, the luscious heat of his breaths against the skin of my abdomen, the smoldering whip of his tongue against my center, the rasp of his whiskers against my tender flesh. I squirm, my body moving of its own volition. His rough hands hold my hips still as he devours me, licking, kissing, nibbling, and when he thrusts a single finger inside me, I go off.

"Please," the pleading moan erupts from my mouth, and at my plea, West moves up my body.

I steal his lips, his breath, but give it back just as quickly as he slides through my wetness and spears into me. The taste of myself on his tongue sends a curl of heat through me. I'm on fire. I'm burning, and I relish in the flames.

Yes. This is what I wanted. His rough palms burrow underneath me, wrapping me in his arms, caging me in the very best way as he thrusts into me. Rolling my hips, I meet him stroke for furiously delicious stroke, watching his face, watching the way his brow puckers, the way his mouth falls open as the phase comes over me and I rake my fangs up his neck. His eyes flash black again, and his fangs snap down.

"Yessss," I hiss, and he gives me one smoldering kiss before he strikes—the sharp sting of the cutting edge of his teeth biting into the meat of my shoulder is everything.

It's warmth and strength and love. It's home.

I've been missing my home for so long. But now, I have it.

WEST AND I ARE SITTING IN MY ENORMOUS BATHTUB, AND I think it is hilarious that my big, sexy, damn-near-seven-foot-tall mate is taking a bubble bath with me. I can't quit giggling as he runs his fingertips up and down my legs. I feel light, as if a huge boulder of grief has been lifted off my chest.

I miss my parents. It hurts me that they missed out on seeing us bonded, but maybe they sent us the shoves we needed to get our collective heads pulled from our asses. I turn in West's lap, slipping in the suds to face him. I study his face—shoulder-length black hair soaked and dripping tiny rivulets of water down his pecs, strong brow, sexy lumberjack beard over an exceedingly strong jaw. And those eyes—such an indeterminate green, anywhere between jade and emerald with every different shade in between.

I love those eyes. I love how expressive they are, how they tell a story without him ever having to say a word. I open my mouth to tell him how happy I am, and although it is probably unnecessary, I do it anyway.

"I am ridiculously, obnoxiously happy right now," I whisper.

A smile blooms over his face, and the curl of his lips tipping up winds its way around my heart.

"That's good, Angel. I'm happy, too," his gruff murmur vibrates through me, and I can't help but slide up his body to kiss him.

And we were so happy. For a while.

19

THAT'S THE THING ABOUT HAPPINESS—IT BLINDS YOU. IT makes you think that everything will be okay, that everything won't eventually go to shit. In my life, I have had very few moments of goodness interspersed with long, dragging years of awful. My few moments of happiness would be the times I've been wrapped around the beautiful Angel currently nestled in my arms.

So, naturally, some asshole has to ruin it.

The ruination comes in the form of a fist pounding on our bedroom door at three-motherfucking-thirty in the morning. Evangeline is straight up dead to the world, and even though the person knocking might actually be using a battering ram instead of a fist, she isn't waking up for anything. A surge of masculine pride hits me as I remember all the dirty things I did to her last night, and I can't help but chuckle as I slide out from underneath her to search for some clothes.

The last four months with Evangeline have been the best of my entire life. While there has always been a niggle of fear in the back of my mind, it isn't for her or us. It is the lingering questions we still have, the fear that Nicola still hasn't been found, and we don't know what really happened there. There is a tense sort of camaraderie we have with the Shifters and Warlocks, but the Witches are less than pleased with us.

And our own kind...

We have many supporters—the working class and regular folk love us because we are cracking down on all of the bullshit from John's reign. Shit I had no idea about. Shit that Walter and a few of his cronies were in on. The head families—except for the Garrison's and Stein's—have been a headache, but nothing we can't handle.

But there is unrest. A sense that something bigger is out there. Something we aren't seeing. Fuck dropping, the proverbial shoe is about to plant itself in our asses. I just know it.

I slip my naked ass into a pair of worn jeans that

were slung over a dark purple velvet bench sitting at the end of our bed. The room is decorated in every single color of the rainbow, and is probably the girliest fucking room I've ever been in, but I don't really care. I give Angel shit for it, but only because I love it when she gets riled.

I zip but forego the button because I'm just going to take these damn jeans off as soon as I can get rid of whoever has the death wish beating on our door.

"Are you kidding me?" I whisper to Aidan as I open the bedroom door.

It takes me a second to realize he's not alone, and when I see Kyle a cold pit of dread hits me in the stomach.

"Fates, man," I mutter as give him a quick slap on the back in greeting. "What happened?"

It has been months since I've seen Kyle, and by the look of him, those months were not spent happy. He isn't as gaunt as he was in Walter's dungeon, but Kyle isn't as healthy as he used to be. His beard is trimmed, his hair tamed, but I can tell he hasn't been eating or consuming as he should.

And his eyes... His eyes are haunted.

"We need to wake Evan. I'm not saying this shit twice," his gruff voice orders, and I resist the urge to punch him in his dumbfuck face because I know he has to be going through some shit.

If he were anyone else, his face would be meeting the Carrera marble floor. Yeah, I'm new to this King shit, but still.

Kyle turns and walks woodenly toward the living area, and I look to Aidan. "You know anything?" I ask.

"Not a thing, man. He's been like a ghost trying to find her," Aidan says as he shakes his head.

"Go watch him and call in Mena, at least. If he has info on Nicola, she'll want to know. We can pass on anything pertinent to everyone else."

"You know good and well Aurelia will kick my ass if she finds out I called her sister and not her. It doesn't matter if she's in her third trimester with twins or not."

"Whatever, man. I need to wake up my woman. Go do what you need to."

I slip back into our room to the closet as I button my jeans. Rifling through the drawers, I find a t-shirt and some socks and grab my boots, and head back to my Angel. She hasn't moved a millimeter from where I left her. I brush my fingertips down her spine as I sit in the open space at her hip, loving that she squirms in her sleep at my touch. I lean down to kiss her shoulder blade, and as the rasp of my beard against her skin, her eyes flutter open.

"Mmm... sleepy. You can do naughty things to me later," she mumbles.

"Angel, you need to wake up. Kyle is here."

Her eyes flash open.

"Are you serious?" she asks not waiting for my response before she hauls ass to the closet to get dressed. I have never been more glad that I can see in the dark as I watch her pert bottom race across the room. She comes back moments later hopping as she pulls up a pair of jeans, and I'm treated to the luscious jiggle of her breasts before she shrugs into a bra and tugs a tank top over her head. I follow her into the bathroom where she throws her hair up in a ponytail, and I brush my teeth as she furiously brushes hers.

"Do you know what's going on?" she asks around her toothbrush, foam coating her mouth.

"Nope," I say after I spit.

"It's going to be bad, isn't it?" she replies grimacing.

I rinse and spit, and turn to look at her, wiping my mouth with the hand towel.

"Probably, Angel, but you know what?" I murmur as I walk on my still bare feet across the tile to wrap her up in my arms.

"What?" she whispers back.

"We'll make it through, you and me. No matter what."

"Promise?" she murmurs her question as her eyes fix on my lips.

When the smile hits my mouth, her lips curl up in response. I give her a hot, wet kiss full of promises I intend on keeping as soon as we're alone again and tug her out of our room and down the hallway to a living room full of people.

Curiously, Aurelia is already here and propped up on the couch with every throw pillow at her disposal, ice water in a glass with a straw and every man in the house willing and ready to do her bidding.

None of this surprises me.

Aurelia has a habit of knowing things long before anyone else, and it is standard operating procedure to cater to a woman with child. Pregnant women—at least in Wraith culture—are considered close to deities. It is so rare for Wraith females to conceive, we as a species are hardwired to accommodate our women. And a woman pregnant with multiples? Forget about it. It doesn't matter that Aurelia is a Phoenix or that she's carrying Phoenix babies. She's more one of us than her own kind anyway.

Asher, Carver, Ian, Aidan, Cam and Rhys all stand in her orbit, with Mena holding her left hand. Evan tells me Aurelia has had a relatively easy pregnancy, so I don't know if she's drawing on Mena's power or if she's just cuddling with her sister. Evan leaves me to go to Aurelia's right side, not only kicking Rhys out of his spot but also taking Aurelia's water from her and putting it on the coffee table so she can hold her hand.

I forget that Nicola is Aurelia and Mena's cousin, and although their relationship is tenuous at best, they must care about her.

"Alright, out with it. What are we dealing with here?" Evangeline orders Kyle, and he flinches as if struck.

Oh, shit. It is going to be so much worse than I thought.

"I-I found her," he begins, "She and that guy Devereux have been hopping from one place to another. Hopping all over the damn planet. St-stealing children from families, teenagers, preschoolers, b-babies..." He pauses then to put a hand over his mouth. "I tried. I tried to get them back. To follow them to keep the chil-dren alive. But I lost her so many times, and I... She's holed up in some abandoned mansion in the wilds of Maine or some shit. Th-there are graves." He stops abruptly—choking on his emotion, on his realization that he has to put a stop to a woman that his body is trained to love, that his soul recognizes as his own.

The guilt he must feel bringing this to us, I cannot fathom.

"When you... when you stop her, can you make sure it doesn't hurt? Can you... It isn't her fault. It's the dirty fucking soul they stuck in her. It isn't her. Just don't... Don't make it hurt, okay?" he pleads searching Evangeline's face for sympathy, but it isn't her who speaks up.

It's me.

"Yes. I can make it painless," I admit, and even though I hate bringing up my past, it's true I can do that. Especially for him.

"It can't be you. Nic told me before this happened. She said that the only way for Iva to be killed was if Evangeline did it. It was one of the last things she told me before I was captured. And I-I want your word you'll... you'll..."

Evangeline leaves her perch on the couch to sit next to Kyle and wraps her arms around his shoulders. She whispers in his ear, and tears start falling from the big man's eyes.

"I just have one question. Are you bound?" she asks, the question we've all been hesitant to ask.

No one wants to kill one just to lose another. No one wants to lose Kyle too.

Kyle shakes his head, and I didn't realize I was holding my breath for the answer to that question until a sigh of relief gusts past my parted lips. I've known

Kyle Brennan for three centuries. Losing him would be a blow.

"She wouldn't let me. Never said why, but I figure she knew this might happen," he croaks, his face destroyed.

It wouldn't matter if I lost Evangeline before I bound her or not—it would still probably kill me. It would just take longer.

"We'll be humane about it, but it needs to happen. Iva won't stop, and if she hasn't already, she's about to start a war," Evangeline says carefully, looking Kyle right in the eye.

His expression is somewhere between ravaged and dead. He is giving up so much.

"I'll tell you where they are, but you'll have to get in on your own. I can't help you kill her," he responds.

So, we make a plan and pray no one dies.

And I've never been more scared in my whole life.

20

EVAN

WE COULDN'T JUST WALK UP TO THE FRONT DOOR LIKE A troop of girl scouts selling cookies and politely ask, *'Hey will you guys just sit still while we kill you?'*

We needed to prepare. Step one was getting the amulets we needed to keep Iva out of our business and out of our minds. Aurelia, being the only one of us with a Witch in her pocket, offered to be the one to get them. Aurelia's tattoo artist friend, Max, was a very nice Witch who didn't prescribe to the old ways. She did things her way and had a different method of doing magic. And an added plus, she hated Tessa with a fiery passion, so my trust in her increased by at least ten-fold. Aurelia and Rhys left to make the short trip to her studio to procure the amulets while the rest of us got the rundown of the grounds from Kyle.

"From what I saw, there is only two ways into the house," Kyle instructs from his seat at the kitchen island as he points to a rough pen and ink rendering of a rather stately—if dilapidated—mansion. The drawing is dirt-stained and crumpled, but it looks as if he had given great care to it. He'd obviously been watching them for a while. The biggest asset with the 'plan' is the massive cliff the house sits on. Surrounded by a thick alpine terrain, the cover will be easy, and the cliff limits egress. Granted, Devereux can travel away at any time, but I have the distinct feeling he won't want to leave his mistress. That's what she has to be, right? I mean, why else would he summon her from Hell?

The plan feels too easy, too clean, and I'm scared.

What if she knows what we're doing? What if she has control over him? What if this is one huge trap? I startle when a scalding hand closes over my shoulder. I look up and back to Mena, who is watching me with concern.

"You can do this, you know. Nicola said it herself— told me you were the only one of us that could," she says encouragingly, but even she is wary of this plan.

I can see it in her eyes.

"That doesn't mean we won't lose people along the way," I whisper back. "This feels too fucking easy."

And it is. There is no way we're just walking up there and doing what we need to without some serious repercussions.

"And it may very well be harder than he's portraying it to be, and we may lose loved ones. But can you live with yourself if she kills another child? This isn't a wait-and-see situation. We know she is actively killing children, and if it is anything like the Aegis genocide..." she breaks off as she swallows thickly. "She won't stop. Not until we make her stop."

I stop my freak out at the wisdom of her words. No, I can't sit idly by while she kills again. Not while I am possibly in a position to stop it. It would be worse than San Francisco. It would be the worst stain on my soul because neglecting this wouldn't be an accident. Letting these children die would be on purpose. And that is the worst sin—not stepping in when I could help save a life.

I look across the island and catch West's eyes. His face looks like it must match mine—blind fear mixed with resignation. I tip my head to signal for him to follow me and start walking toward the hallway. When we're out of earshot, I ask him, "What do you think?"

"I'm thinking body armor. Lots and lots of body armor. And if I thought it would work, and those bastards wouldn't just travel out of there, a grenade launcher," he says matter-of-factly.

"But you want to go, right?"

"Fuck, yes, I want to go. Not want, Angel, we need to go. And as much as I don't want you to be in harm's way, you have to go too. I know you don't know much about my childhood, but... My father was the Devil himself. The things he did... no one should have to endure. I cannot stand for murder, but when it's kids..." he trails off shaking his head.

I step into his space and wrap my arms around him.

"One of these days, you're going to have to tell me about your life, my love. Not today, but someday, this info would be good to know. I don't even know if you want children of your own."

"Of course I want children. Girls with your beautiful face or little boys with your eyes. I'm not picky. Whether it is one or ten, I don't mind either, but I'd like more than one. We're both only children, and I'd love our kid to have a sibling. I'm actually amazed it took you four months to ask that."

"I didn't want to push. I figured we had time. But the bad stuff—even the not so bad stuff—I'd like to know, my love. You've carried it too long, I think."

I get an affirmative grunt and a squeeze in response. I know it will take some hounding, but I'll get at least some of it from him. West has held that horribly toxic poison in his chest for centuries.

Maybe one of these days he'll let it go.

That thought passes through my brain at the same instant the front door opens, and Aurelia and Rhys walk through it. Well, Aurelia waddles through it, but whatever. Her waddle is slight, but the woman is carrying twins, so naturally I have to give her shit.

"What's up, Mama Duck?" I say with a snicker.

"Fuck you," she replies with a baleful expression on her face.

Touchy, touchy. She adjusts the short jean jacket that covers her arms, and fiddles with the black crepe sundress that flows over her ripe belly.

"Aww, come on, you waddle and have feathers. You're more than halfway there," I giggle.

"Seriously. I will make Rhys kill you. Don't test the limits of my friendship, woman," she says, but I know she's just fucking with me.

Aurelia is warily excited about her pregnancy, and has been taking every precaution so her babies turn out healthy. Sparing, no; katas, yes. Junk food, no; fruit and veg, yes. Over-training, no; resting when needed, yes. In the beginning, she over trained and fought and exposed herself to the elements, but now, she does everything she can to be safe. I think it is because she's scared she'll lose them, and with her history, I don't blame her.

"Fine, Sensitive Sally, I'll quit fucking with you. Max help us out?" I ask.

"Yep. You already have one—Max told me she saw one around your neck the last time you came with me to the shop—which explains so freaking much, BTW. She was in a rush so she didn't make one for me, Mena, Rhys or you because we didn't need them. Rhys, because he's not going with you and me and Mena because our Aegis protects us. Everyone else gets one," she informs me as she raises a censuring eyebrow.

Busted. It's been a century and Aurelia didn't know about my little blue amulet. Well, she knows now.

"What? A girl has to have her secrets," I shrug, unapologetic.

"Yeah, yeah. You say that now. What happens when you're in trouble? Huh? I can't see shit with that fucking thing on. It's annoying."

"Yeah, yeah. I'll be fine."

"Whatever, pass these out, and make sure Kyle gets one. I have a feeling he'll be an easy mark for her to tap into," she says as she hands me the pouch of amulets in her hand.

"Good idea," I say as we walk into the kitchen.

A kitchen that doesn't have a Kyle perched at a barstool.

"Where's Kyle?" West rumbles behind me.

"He just smoked out..." Cam answers bewildered.

"Oh, son of a fucking bitch. He. Did. Not," Aurelia curses as her eyes begin to glow. "He did. That stupid motherfucker!"

"He went to her, didn't he?" West asks.

"Of course he did, the moron. Is he trying to get you killed?" she replies.

"No. He's trying to say goodbye. I would probably do the same," he returns gruffly. "If you only had minutes with Rhys, wouldn't you?"

Her eyes stop glowing, and she takes a good long look at him. "Probably, but that fucks with your timeline. You guys need to go as soon as possible to try and intercept him."

"Alright, everyone. Get your shit squared away and be ready in ten," West orders and they move.

The King has spoken.

First, mid-March in northern Maine is cold as fuck. Second, the nighttime temperatures make the daytime temps look like summer. I wish I would have brought a parka. I thought Colorado was chilly, but I had no idea.

This is not the excellent Colorado weather. This is windy hell on a stick.

The forest gives adequate cover, but the early morning hours are working against us. I would have preferred to attack under the cover of darkness, but Kyle royally screwed our timeline. I find it hard to be angry with him. If I only had one single day left with West, I couldn't say how rational I'd be.

We traveled in about a mile out from the house, checking for traps, surveillance and the like, but finding none. It's like they want us to come—either that or they think they aren't going to be caught. I don't know which option scares me more.

The trees are dense right up next to the small yard in front of the house, and the bellows of the ocean rushing against the cliffs the only sounds.

No birds. No crickets. No animals.

It is the calm before the storm. I feel it and so does everyone else, this electric charge in the air like just before a lightning strike. The pressure, the oppressive weight of the air sticks to us. I'm just behind West when I feel a stir. I don't think anything of it at first until I catch a glimpse of Mena.

She wasn't phased a moment ago, but she is now,

and despite the blue flames that lick her skin and the brilliantly bright blue wings that are spread wide, she is white as a sheet. Her fingertips crackle like tiny lightning rods, and her head is cocked to one side as if she's listening to something only she can hear.

While she's frozen, all hell seems to break out around us. Men file out of the front door of the house while barrels of rifles peek out of the upper floor windows. The world explodes as bullets whiz past us, but I'm not watching them. I'm watching Mena's face because she knows something. Something horrible is happening, and I don't know what it is, but I know it's bad.

Her eyes meet mine.

"Aurelia is in trouble. I have to go," she whispers, and I have no idea how I hear her with the guns firing and men fighting around us.

She pulls a katana from her back in a quick, seamless motion and cuts down the Wraith barreling for her, practically cutting him in two. She cuts down two more before she grabs Asher, and they smoke out of the forest leaving us to this Hell to go to a new one with her sister, my best friend.

Fates, we're too late.

21

AURELIA

I thought I was safe, thought not going into battle with them would make it so. While I regretted not going to help, I knew I wasn't going to waddle my seven-and-a-half-months-pregnant ass onto the battlefield and do anything of consequence. I would be in the way, and I would put my babies lives and my husband's life at risk. But while I was worrying about my friends—no, my family—I should have been worrying about my babies, my husband, myself.

I'd wanted to stay at the penthouse. It was Evangeline's headquarters after all, and I figured this would be the place everyone would head to once the dust was settled.

The pregnancy had been easier than I thought it would be. Sure, I was always hot—even in the dead of winter—I couldn't see my feet anymore, and shaving my legs had become a real problem, but my babies were thriving. Only six more weeks to go until they were considered full term and then I would get my lovelies. We have no idea what gender or genders are cooking in there, and since we have no way to know, we did the nursery in neutral colors.

Rhys has been my rock, dealing with my crazy ass while I try to navigate the emotions of guilt and fear. Losing my first child was the worst thing to ever happen to me. More than the torture or losing Lucien or losing my mind to Iva. Losing my first baby was the absolute worst thing, and because of that, I have been either in denial about this pregnancy or running to the end of the spectrum and worrying about every action, morsel of food, and drop of water I've put in my body. I have been a mess, but Rhys... Rhys has been happy—so stinking ecstatic—he's willfully getting every ounce of baby gear set up and ready. It's like he's the one nesting and not me.

But losing the babies is my worst nightmare. Failing to protect my first child has always been my greatest sin. Failing to protect these children would kill me.

"You doing okay, Gorgeous?" Rhys' honey-over-gravel voice calls from my right.

I break my gaze on the lone brilliant sapphire blue amulet sitting on the island to look at him.

"Yeah, why?"

"You stopped in the middle of heading to the bathroom to stare at the amulet, babe," he says as he rubs me between my shoulder blades. His touch is comforting and sets my mind back to rights, but I feel a niggle of fear.

"I... I don't like not being able to see. I don't like not being able to warn them if I can. I don't like those amulets," I mutter.

"Yeah, I know you hate not knowing shit ahead of time, but they need the protection of them, so do your best not to worry. Mena is with them, and she'll help them if not win, then definitely survive."

"You're right. I know you're right, but I can't help but feel... like something is wrong, and I'm not sure if it is them or the babies or us. I feel off, and I want to grab a weapon, and I want to eat my weight in cheesecake. What the hell is wrong with me?" I ask as I turn away from him, but he comes up behind me and wraps one arm around my chest and puts one large hand over my belly.

It might be weird or trite or whatever, but when he

puts a hand over the babies it calms me down so fast, he might as well have shot me with a tranq dart. I cover his hand with both of mine, and one of the babies kicks me. Hard.

I should have listened to my gut.

I should have, but I didn't.

So when the five Wraiths smoke into the room, I don't realize my worst nightmare is coming to life until it is.

WEST

Things are going from okay, to not good, to *we're gonna to die* so fast, I don't know what to do. My first thought is how many minions does this woman have? For fuck's sake, is she that good at brainwashing people or is she just that good at bargaining lives she doesn't have to? It isn't just Wraiths fighting for her either—which doesn't make a lick of sense to me at all. She was the one who ordered the mass killings of so many of our families. She was the one who had our houses and lives burned to ashes. Why would they fight for this woman?

I see a few Phoenixes out here, their Fireskin glowing orange in the early morning light. I don't understand that either. How could someone who was destined for sending souls to a better place, hurt and kill so many? Wouldn't they want to go to the same place they sent so many souls to? Wouldn't they fear Hell that much more because they knew what they'd be missing?

I'm between the house and Evangeline, but that doesn't mean a single thing right now. We're surrounded by men and bullets are whizzing by our heads from the open second-floor windows. Evangeline drops to the bracken of the forest floor to return fire, taking out two of the three before she concentrates on the Wraith in front of her. Aidan and Cam are on her like white on rice, guarding her back as they eliminate threat after threat trying to take out my Angel while I'm stuck separated from her.

Good men.

They can't stop them all, though, and I've never been more glad that she'd spent so much time training to fight. She's fluid and beautiful as she spins, and if she weren't beheading a man with a rapier in the middle of a dicey as hell fight, I'd want to kiss her. But for now, I'm stuck in a well-matched battle with a man just as big as I am. Every strike has a parry, every slice has a block, and I can't seem to get the upper hand on him.

When the slice to my back comes, it's a shock. I was so engrossed in my Angel and the man in front of me who I just can't seem to kill, I missed the man behind me. The blow takes me to my knees.

Now I have two Wraiths bearing down on me.

RHYS

I have never been more glad that I never leave the house without at least one weapon than I am right now. Five Wraiths smoke into the penthouse, and I could kick myself for not taking Aurelia seriously before. When has she ever been wrong about her fears?

That's right, never.

I pull my H&K from my spine holster and fire a round as I yank Aurelia behind me. The first one goes down easy, but when I have my whole world behind me, any threat at all is too much. Then, she isn't behind me anymore. Aurelia's hand rips from mine, and she's dragged away by a Witch I didn't see before. The Witch looks so much like Tessa, if I hadn't watched her die with my own eyes, I would have believed it was her. Aurelia jerks from the woman's hold, but she is unbalanced and falls to all fours just missing the coffee table by mere inches. She seems unhurt at the moment, but all I want to do is kill the Witch who took her from me.

I'm torn, but I shouldn't have been. Aurelia isn't helpless despite her delicate condition. She reaches underneath the skirt of her dress to a thigh bandolier filled with throwing knives. She makes short work of the Witch's Achilles tendon, and then to add insult to injury, Aurelia embeds the knife in the Witch's thigh. In the melee of her screams of agony I take out another Wraith, but my good luck soon runs out.

In the next instant, my left shoulder is struck by a bullet. I don't feel it, but Aurelia's shriek of pain sends the worst sort of fear through me.

If I bleed, she bleeds. If I die, she dies. The babies. The babies.

MENA

I didn't know when I started feeling when Aurelia was in trouble—birth maybe—but it was never this acute. Never this visceral. It was more than just knowing. I felt her fear, her pain. I felt it more than my own and I knew —I knew it was her. It had to be. My left shoulder was on fire, and I could barely keep hold of the Glock in my hand, but I hadn't been struck. Ash was right next to me, and since I'd learned how to shield him as well as myself, I knew he wasn't injured.

My gut said it was her, and I knew I couldn't wait. I knew she had no time. So I met Evan's eyes with apology in mine. Because I couldn't do what I said I would do. I couldn't fulfill my promise to Nicola. I had to leave them. I had to go to Aurelia. Because if I didn't, she would die.

"Aurelia is in trouble. I have to go," I whisper as I grab Asher's hand.

"We have to go back. Now," I tell him.

He doesn't question why, he doesn't do anything but grab my waist and travel from the battlefield back to the penthouse, trading one Hell for another. I reinforce the shield around myself and Ash, and when we reform in the middle of the kitchen, I am supremely glad I had the forethought. Otherwise, Ash would have a bullet in his brain right about now.

Splashes of blood and gore litter the kitchen. A body of a Wraith lay just in front of the sink and another in the dining room. A Witch is screaming of revenge and agony in the living room, and Rhys is trying to protect Aurelia with his body as three Wraiths advance on him. I blink, and Ash has taken out one of the men, but the other prove much harder to kill.

These men are not the untrained peons Walter offered up for slaughter. These men are killers.

I catch movement in the living room just as the two Wraiths make their move. The Witch is crawling for Aurelia, her fingertips glowing red with unspent magic. I do the only thing I can think of, I throw a bolt of my Aegis at her, knocking her into the thick floor to ceiling glass window so hard the three-inch pane cracks. The light in her eyes goes out as blood pours from her eyes, nose, ears, and mouth. Her death was too quick for someone who would hurt a pregnant woman, and I wish I'd killed her slower.

Bloodthirsty, perhaps, but I don't give a fuck.

Ash eliminates one of the two Wraiths still left standing, but we have a bigger problem. The last one has dragged Aurelia away from Rhys and has positioned her in front of him like a shield. The worst part isn't that he's using my sister's pregnant body for his own cowardice.

No, the worst part is the loaded gun he has against her temple.

EVAN

I feel it before I see it—the imminent danger West is in. It is a niggle in the back of my mind and swoop to my gut. I turn in time to see a giant of a man slash a thick sword upward, and the way West's back arches, the blade hit its target.

He's down on all fours. He's breathing, but he's not moving. He's not getting to his feet. *He's hurt. Oh, shit.*

My brain blanks for a split second and then regroups. I embed my rapier in the gut of the closest enemy and slash outward, spilling his innards all over the forest floor. The Wraith's eyes turn from smug to shocked, and I watch his expression go slack with a fucking smile on my face. His death will be slow and painful, and it is a slight comfort to me that I make sure the killers of children leave this world screaming.

I smoke out from my spot of relative safety between Cam and Aidan and go to West. I feel my power rise in my chest as I move, and when I travel to the place just before them, the men fly back as if pulled by a puppeteer's string. I move to them and take their heads with my rapier before they even knew what hit them. I move to the next and the next and the next until there are no more lives for me to take outside.

When Nicola steps out on the wide wrap-around porch, I have to remind myself that it isn't her. That the betrayal I feel at the sight of her face isn't real. I have to remind myself that she has Iva's dark soul squatting inside her like a toad. It is easier than I'd thought to separate the two, especially when she drags a bleeding Kyle across the porch planks from behind her like a rag doll.

Nicola wouldn't do that to him. I saw her with Kyle months ago—before all this mess. I saw her expressions. I saw how she felt even before he did. Nicola was taken by the giant man from the start.

She flings Kyle's broken but still breathing body from her fingertips as if he were a piece of errant trash. Kyle lands at my feet, and I feel more than see the rest of my family file in around me. Her expression flickers for a moment, but when this woman talks, Iva's thick, Irish brogue slips from her lips.

"Evangeline, dearie. I've been expecting you."

22

MENA

I don't know what to do.

I'm stuck here watching my larger than life sister shiver in fear. No, not shiver—she's vibrating, she's so scared. Scared because anything he does to her, he does to her entire family. Her husband, her babies. Aurelia's eyes pale, pupilless eyes are wide and rivulets of tears are falling from them. Her left shoulder is bloody and limp at her side, and her chest is heaving with panicked breaths.

I have to figure out what to do. If I shock him, his muscles could tense, and he could pull the trigger by accident.

Then, out of the corner of my eye I see Aurelia's

fingers tiptoe down her right leg as she pulls up the fabric of her dress to reveal her thigh bandolier filled with throwing knives. I make no movement, nothing to give away her actions because the Wraith holding her looks skittish at best. His eyes dart at the three of us— three fully phased predators ready to skin him alive at the first available opportunity.

I glance at Rhys and Ash out of the corner of my eye. It is amazing to me that these two men who couldn't be more different, have matching expressions of wrath on their faces. Rhys' Fireskin paints him in an orange glow, his black and blood-red wings spread wide, his face a promise of retribution. Ash's phase has turned his ice-blue eyes black, talons longer than Aurelia's throwing knives curl from his fingertips, two-inch-long upper and lower fangs give him a macabre smile, and his power sweeps around him in swaths of black smoke.

It's good we look so deadly. It's keeping the Wraith's fearful eyes on us instead of on the woman in his arms. The woman who at this very moment decides it is high time he feels what Fireskin does to people who fuck with us. Bright orange flames skate over Aurelia's skin, burning the Wraith's arms, face and torso. He flinches back, howling in agony and Aurelia shoves her knife into the soft spot just under the man's chin. The blade isn't long enough to kill him, but that doesn't matter.

She takes her burning hand and grabs his jaw as she rips out the knife.

She gives him a look that would strike the fear of God into anyone, but at this point, the man shouldn't fear God—he should fear her. With a hideous snarl, she flips the blade to an overhand grip and drives home into his eye. She holds him up until he quits twitching and then drops him like a smoldering sack of potatoes at her feet.

We're all ready to go to her—ready to check her over until she doubles over in pain as she clutches her belly.

The babies.

EVAN

It is the worst trick in the book to take away someone's will—to take away everything that they are and make them a puppet. Iva has been doing it for centuries under the radar, but never this overt, never killing so indiscriminately, never.

Nicola's body is merely a suit that Iva is wearing. Her voice is different, her mannerisms are different, but the most startling, is her eyes. Nicola's eyes are an unseeing cornflower blue, but Aurelia told me that Iva used brown glass eyes in the place of her missing ones. And though Nicola's eyes were never taken from her because she was born blind, the woman before me possesses an odd honey-brown set of peepers.

Her hair is down, flowing around her shoulders and down her back and she's weirdly wearing makeup—something Nicola neither wears nor has to wear. What is she getting ready for, a fucking party?

She's been expecting me.

Sure. I'll bet she has. I look at Kyle who is struggling to his feet, and realize she has beaten him almost senseless. Well, check one item off my list. West reaches out a hand to help him up, and he shakily makes it to his feet.

"Please, Nic. Please make it back to us. Please," Kyle rasps.

Iva's girlish giggle in response turns my stomach.

"And why would she do that when I am here now? Nicola Miller was a poor blind girl who never did anything but try and scheme her way around me. Now that I'm here, there is no need for her to wonder. She is powerless. There is only me now," she says as she smiles.

Her pronouncement sends a chill down my spine. I held out hope that Nicola was still in there. Still fighting. But I don't know if she is. I don't know if there is anything left of Nicola to fight.

It makes me want to break my promise to Kyle. It makes me want to make her suffer like Nicola has, like we all have. I want to, but I won't. I may have taken lives, but I am nothing like this woman. I don't have this level of evil in me. I don't need power or subjugation. I need love and support and friends—and these are things I have already. These are things Iva will never have because as much power as she scrabbles to possess, she will never have it all.

That thought brings a smile to my face, making the smug one on her face droop a bit. I adjust my hold on my rapier and pull my tri-dagger from its sheath.

"Where's your minion, Iva? Doesn't he want to play?" I taunt.

"Oh, don't you worry your pretty head about him, darling. He's doing exactly what he's supposed to do," she counters and then her Fireskin explodes over her flesh and Nicola's brilliant orange wings burst from her back.

As she takes her first step off the porch stair, fire catches in her wake—jumping from plank to plank, setting the house ablaze.

RHYS

The pain on her face.

Fates, please. Please don't do this to us. It's too early, too early for them. There's something wrong.

I'm proved right when a small puddle of blood starts forming at her feet. It happens in slivers of seconds. The agony on her face morphs into shock. Then her Fireskin dies, and Aurelia's face turns white. Then her eyes roll back in her head as she collapses. Asher moves the quickest of us all and catches her before she hits the ground. He is gentle, but there isn't much that can stop the hurt to her poor body.

Mena places a hand on her belly, and already I can tell Aurelia is drawing on her. Drawing so much of her, her fire goes out as well. Then, Mena's face drains of color, blood running from her nose.

Fates, please.

"T-the hos-hospital in Knoxville. With the W-witches. Go, Ash. Now," Mena orders haltingly.

He meets my eyes, and I can see the fear in them. Fear for his wife, fear for mine, and fear for our lives. He gives me a nod and gathers Aurelia in his arms as he smokes out of the room—carrying my whole world in his arms as he goes.

WEST

The large sprawling porch blazes bright as the flames jump from the steps to the external walls and filter down to the dry forest bracken beneath our feet. We have to move. We have to hurry before we burn. But Evangeline doesn't pay any mind to the flames that will surely burn her or the woman in front of her. My Angel's shoulders set, her jaw clenches and the phase she was holding back flows over her like water.

She moves slightly as if she is about to make her away across the flames to Iva, but before she can make it an inch, black smoke of a traveling Wraith comes in behind her. Time moves like molasses. I won't make it in time to stop them, but I go to her anyway.

Please, no. Please, not my Angel.

I may not be in time, but someone else is. Kyle shoves Evangeline out of the way as he takes the blade meant for her back in his gut. Devereux Emerson looks slightly put out by this turn of events and uses his boot to shove him off his blade.

By the time Kyle's body meets the earth, Devereux is stuck like a hog on a spit by the blades of Cam, Aidan, Carver, Ian, and myself. Ian wrenches out his blade first as he drops to help Kyle, and the rest of us follow suit, but it is only I who raise my blade again. Devereux's body is pouring blood, but he's still breathing, his eyes rolling like a spooked mare.

He is a threat we have to eliminate, and I'm not waiting for this fucker to figure out a way to resurrect himself a second time. No. Fuck that. I take my kukri and remove his head with one quick strike. I don't wait to transport his sorry ass right where it belongs. Opening my jaws, I inhale his soul as quickly as I can, shutting my mind off to the haunting images that filter through my brain of every horrendous sin he's committed.

The scream coming from Nicola's body sends a chill of fear down my spine. My eyes shoot up from the man who almost took my life to the woman trying to take my Angel's.

23

ASHER

I SHOULDN'T BE THE ONE TO DO THIS. I SHOULDN'T BE THE ONE holding this much responsibility. The only thing in my life that hasn't gone to shit is Mena. The only family I have is the one I made for myself, and I can't be the one to ruin it. I shouldn't be the one holding something so precious.

But I am, and there is no one else who could do it. Mena looked like the life was draining out of her, and if she's that bad, I cannot begin to wrap my mind around what Aurelia's body is going through. She is dead weight in my arms, her jacket and dress soaked in blood as I hold her tight to me and travel to the one hospital I know where we would be accepted.

When I make it to the emergency room entrance, a Shifter I recognize from months ago is waiting for me right outside along with three Witches. The Shifter looks to be the leader of this group and asks me questions rapid fire as I set Aurelia's limp body on a gurney, and the three Witches move as if their hair is on fire, booking it to the operating room elevators. All I can focus on are Aurelia's feet, which are shod in thin-soled sandals that used to be tan leather but are now stained black with blood. My eyes well with tears and as the elevator door close on those feet, the first tears of worry and fear fall.

I feel a pull on my elbow, and I glance back to the Shifter female. I notice right away the color of her hair. It is an odd color that danced back and forth between brown and red.

"What's your name, sir?" the Shifter's voice is calm, and that scares me worse than anything.

"Asher. My name is Asher."

"Okay, Asher, I'm Willa. I need you to tell me what's going on," she orders, her no-nonsense voice waking me up a bit.

"They were attacked. She's—Aurelia—is seven and a half months pregnant with twin Phoenixes. She started bleeding from between her legs... There was a Witch, I don't know if she did a spell. Her fingers were glowing red, and then Aurelia was bleeding. I don't know. I don't know," I say, and I notice she's had my arm in hers as she's leading me to the same elevator Aurelia just went to. I yank my arm from hers and take a step back.

"I-I have to get my wife. I have to get her husband. I have to... I'll be back. Is there a place where we can arrive without going through the ER?" I ask because I need to get back to them as soon as I can.

"Sure, just travel to the conference room upstairs. But Asher? Get back quick, okay?" Willa's voice is soft but firm, and I know I don't have much time.

"Thanks, Willa," I say as I realize I may never be able to thank this woman for snapping me out of my freak out.

She nods and I travel back to my wife with fear embedded deep in my heart.

EVAN

The howl of agony coming from Nicola's body isn't Iva's. No, this is Nicola's pain erupting from her breast, creating a maelstrom of fear and grief and rage. Her eyes are trained on Kyle, and her fear is palpable. She drops to her knees, scrambling across the forest floor through fire and dirt and bracken, trying to get to him.

I look behind me and order them to get him out of here.

"Get him to a hospital!" I scream rushing to intercept her.

In her shock, her Fireskin has died down, but I don't trust it or her. I strike out with my rapier, putting a thick gash on her cheek, but that doesn't stop her. I restrain her bodily keeping her away from the injured man.

"No! No, don't keep me back from him. Please! Kyle! Please!" she pleads, and the change in her voice from Iva's thick Irish brogue to Nicola's delicate English accent almost make me believe her.

"I'll let you take her soul. I'll hold her back, just please let me say goodbye to him," she begs, her eyes flooded with desperate tears, and I let her go.

She wastes no time with me and shoves past me to get to him. Nicola grabs his face to hurriedly whisper in his ear as Ian tries to staunch the flow of blood pouring from Kyle's stomach. His eyes drift open, and he grasps her wrists.

"Lo-love you, Nic. See you on the other side," Kyle whispers before his eyes roll back in his head, and he loses consciousness.

"Noooooooo!" she shrieks, but Aidan doesn't wait for her to lose it.

He rips Kyle from her arms and travels from the fray

so all she's clutching is air. A rumbled shriek erupts from her chest, her eyes blaze and her Fireskin blooms over her flesh. West and I scramble back from Nicola.

Without Kyle here, without her focus pulled to him, something passes over her face, and I know Iva is back controlling her body.

"You should have killed me when you had the chance, little girl," Iva says as she reaches for me with a lone burning hand.

She misses me by inches as West catches me by the waist and swings me out of the way, accepting the agonizing burn of her touch for himself. He growls in pain before tossing me away from her.

But that's my mate she's fucking with, and I phase without thought or volition. Rushing her without care for my hide or my life. She has West in her clutches, and she's not fucking with one more person I care about. My power swarms through me, the cold blankness causing the earth to shake and debris and dirt and leaves to swirl first around my body, but picking up speed and force and growing, growing, growing until it is bigger than her and me.

This is more than just my life or her life or the lives of my family. This is for the Aegis children she damn near murdered into extinction, the Witch and Warlock and Shifter children that she killed for whatever sick reason she had, for the hurt and pain and suffering she's caused. I make it to her, ripping him from her hands and grabbing her arms in my blistering grip.

Her agony is swift, and though I hate hurting Nicola, I cannot let her get away. I can't let her live after all the death she's caused. Iva's scream turning into Nicola's and it brings me so much pain to do this.

"Ju-just do it, Evan. It always had to be this way. Take the soul, dammit! Do it!"

The permission is what I needed, I think. The knowledge that she knew what I was doing, that she allowed it.

I open my mouth and inhale the dark, twisted essence of Iva and fourteen hundred years of condemning deeds filters through my mind. Murder. Torture. Genocide. And more recently the killing of children with extraordinary powers. The ones who had more power than most. The ones who could be her downfall one day.

And now they never would.

That was the worst because they weren't just teenagers, they were babies, barely a fresh breath in this world before their life was snuffed out. I can't take it. I can't take so much evil... I can't...

Blackness clouds my vision, and I hear my howling scream before I hear nothing at all.

MENA

Asher picked us up and took us to this sterile, silent hospital waiting room where we've been sitting for hours now. I haven't eaten, I have barely moved except for the motion of my nervously shifting feet. Rhys looks like he's about to lose his fucking mind, and all he can do is stare out the window at the rapidly fading day.

Has it only been a day? I've lived almost two centuries, and they have flown by without a word or whisper, but this day? This day has lasted decades, millennia, eons. Aurelia isn't the only person we're waiting on word about. Evan, West, Kyle are all severely injured. Aidan came with Kyle first, and then it was Cam bringing Evan and West hanging onto Ian by a very thin thread.

And Nicola.

We don't know who will be there when she wakes up, or if she even does. Right now I can't think about who she'll be.

I can only think about my sister as I sit here waiting to see if her world will explode once again.

A doctor—Asher called her Willa—passes through the OR automatic doors, and I don't know if I should be pleased or scared, and I don't know how I can breathe right now.

"Aurelia?"

Rhys jumps up from his perch on the windowsill to meet her. His body is strung tight like a string about to snap.

"Your wife is in recovery. Your daughter and son are in the NICU for a little while, but given their species, I don't expect they'll be in there for very long."

"A da-daughter and a son?" Rhys breathes. "Can I see her? Can I see them?"

"Yes to both, but her first, and only one at a time."

"Do you have word on Evangeline, West or Kyle?" Cam asks, his voice a quiet, somber rumble.

Willa looks back at him, and though her eyes flash from amber to green back to amber again, she makes no other outward sign other than a small shake of her head.

"N-not yet," she mutters before leading Rhys away back through the double doors.

Three lives accounted for and three more to go.

I hate waiting.

EVAN

My mind is cotton candy and fluffy clouds, but all I want is clarity. I want to wake up. I want to see my West. My eyelids are heavy, but I force them open. My room is dim, but I can make out the orange blinking lights of a vital sign monitor. Right next to it, sleeping upright in an uncomfortable hospital chair is my West.

Tight black t-shirt over dark-wash jeans and motorcycle boots. His wavy hair is pulled back from his face in a topknot, but his beard is scraggly and unkempt, and I can tell he's been sitting there for quite some time.

His large hand engulfs mine and rests on the bed at my side. I squeeze it before drifting off again, happy he is alive and well, and obviously better off than me if he's out of a hospital bed, but I'm so tired.

"Evangeline? Angel?" his wonderful rumble vibrates through my chest.

"Hmm?" I sleepily respond.

"Never mind, baby. Just sleep."

"Mmmm… only if you come sleep with me. I sleep better with you."

"Whatever you want, Angel," he murmurs, and his warm arms close around me as I drift back to sleep.

And I had sweet dreams.

EPILOGUE

EVAN

"West! We're going to be late!" I yell from my perch at the bathroom vanity. Yes, I might be on hour two of beauty prep, but dammit it isn't every day your best friend in the entire universe decides it is high time to have a wedding.

Aurelia had a bad habit of waiting until the dust is settled to let herself be happy, concentrating on everyone else and solving all the problems before she could move on to her joy, but since the twins were born, she has decided to be happy every day. I've never met a woman more suited for motherhood than my best friend, and as soon as she figures out how to stop swearing in front of the kiddos, she'll be golden.

"All I have to do is shower and put on a suit. I do not have to do makeup and hair for two whole hours that looks like you just rolled out of bed looking that beautiful. Chill, woman," he grumbles as he leans down to kiss the sensitive spot on my neck, the soft yet rough rasp of his beard doing all kinds of awesome things to my belly.

I want to argue, but it's true. All he has to do is put on a suit. And if he doesn't quit it, all my hard work is going to get shot to hell when I attack him. He meets my eyes in the mirror, gives me a chuckle, and then runs his fangs along my shoulder inciting a full body shiver. He turns and walks his naked ass over to the shower. I have to fight all of my instincts so I don't follow him in and ruin my hair. It took me forever to do this damn hair.

When Aurelia said she wanted to be married to Rhys in a meadow, I loved the idea. She said she wanted something simple, nothing too fussy. Just friends and family and Rhys. It sounded good in theory, but Aurelia was the Primary, and she couldn't do something small if she wanted to—too many people would be pissed if they didn't receive an invitation. Mena skated by on her wedding to Asher because she married a Wraith and it is not customary for Wraiths to have wedding ceremonies. Our bindings are rather private, and in our culture, all a person needs to see is the binding mark to know you're taken. That's not to say Mena and Asher didn't have a wedding—they did—but it was a private affair on a secluded beach.

But Aurelia wasn't that lucky. So I took over the planning and flexed my Queen muscle to get shit done. Well, and I had Claire's help. For someone so quiet and reserved, Claire can organize like a boss and scold caterers like it was her job. Ari had her hands full with the babies once they finally came out of the NICU, and is about the least fussy bride I've ever seen in my freaking life. She only cared about her dress and the fact that she was marrying Rhys. Everything else was fair game for me to choose, and I went nuts with the bohemian theme.

My mind drifts to the first time I got to see her after the twins were born. I was up and about before she was, which is a testament to how much childbirth takes you to the edge of death. My body just needed a few days of rest. Aurelia's body needed to heal itself back from the brink of death. Willa never told Rhys how close the doctors were to losing all three of them, and I'm glad they didn't. Rhys was barely hanging on by a thread.

Aurelia was white as a sheet sitting up in her hospital bed. Rhys was in the NICU watching the twins, and she was alone for the first time since they were born. I didn't even get to ask what was wrong.

"I need to ask you a favor," she burst out.

"Of course, anything."

"Can you get West back here? I want to ask you both something."

"Sure thing, darling," I said as I peeked my head out of the room and crooked a finger to West as he rested on the wall just outside the door.

"All present and accounted for, what's up?" I said as I returned.

"I want to run the twins' names past you to get your approval."

"Okay. Shoot," West said, but Ari looked nervous.

"We want our son to be named Henry Alexander Constantine," she said, her eyes on West.

He took a step back in surprise but didn't look angry. I had no idea why the name held significance to him.

"I was born Henry Carmichael Weston, but you knew that already, didn't you?" he rumbled, and I looked at him in surprise.

West didn't talk about his past. He gave me the highlights—enough to know his father was a fucking rat bastard, and his mother, Merina, was one of the strongest women I'd never get to know—but I didn't know what his given name was.

"That I did, and your mother gave you a good first name that I hope you don't mind me borrowing."

"I think that wherever her soul is, she'd love that," he replied, his voice rough with emotion.

"Good," she said taking a deep breath. "We would like to name our daughter Olivia Collette Constantine," she announced, and it was me who took the step back in surprise.

"Yes. Absolutely. Mama would have loved that."

"My babies have names," she whispered to herself. "What do you guys say about taking a field trip to go see them?"

"You allowed to do that, little mama?" West asked.

"Meh, probably not, but I want to tell Rhys the good news, and I want to feed my babies. So I'm going to one way or another. It would just be easier if one of you procured me a wheelchair first."

"Yes, ma'am," he returned as I went to hold her hand.

Aurelia's teary smile made my heart hurt.

"I'll never be able to thank you for all you did for us. You killed the boogeyman, Evangeline, and I'll never be able to tell you how grateful I am. I love you, darling girl," she whispered as she squeezed my hands.

"Love you too. Now let's go see these babies."

And they were the most beautiful babies I'd ever seen. Born at only four pounds, eight ounces for Henry and four pounds, four ounces for Olivia, they were thriving better than I thought they would for being so small. Both babies had a full head of black hair like their momma, but their eyes did not match at all. Baby Livy had her mother's pale, mint-green pupilless eyes, and Henry had his father's dark, coffee-colored ones. It was obvious already that Henry had some Aegis powers. He kept frying the vital sign monitors, so they quit hooking him up to them. Sooner than they thought possible, the twins were cleared to go home.

A smile stretches across my face, and I blink back into the present. I wonder how hard it would be to convince West to knock me up. Meh. I'll wait until I get done christening every room of the penthouse before I do something like that.

I study my hair and makeup in the mirror. My honey blonde and platinum hair was teased out to maximum volume before I braided sections away from my face and then wrapped it all into a delicate chignon at the nape of my neck. My face was done up to full dewy high-lighted awesomeness, and while the look mimicked a 'natural' look, I had more makeup on my face than the law should allow.

West stepped from the shower, still dripping rivulets of water down his tattooed eight-pack leading down his happy trail on down to nirvana.

Hmm. I wonder how bad my hair is going to get messed up when I attack him.

Totally worth the risk.

MENA

Aurelia got ready at my massive master bedroom vanity, her tan skin didn't require much makeup but she still gussied herself up for the big day. Her naturally wavy hair got a stern talking to by a very hot curling iron, and decided to submit to her will and behave for the rest of the day after it was wrestled into submission into a complicated but loose bun at the nape of her neck. Instead of a veil, she wore a beautiful gold leaf hairpin that rested just atop her bun.

Her dress, still on the hanger in my closet waiting for her to finish up, is delicate and ethereal. Full belled sleeves lined with scallops of lace matching the deep open 'V' at the back, full silk organza and scalloped lace skirt with a chapel train. Every time I look at it, I smile. It is so her. Complicated but simple, stylish without giving a fuck. Yep, that's my sister.

"Okay, I'm ready. Where is Evan?" Aurelia calls.

"Never mind. She's going to be five more minutes," she yells answering her own question.

At this point I don't even want to know. I slip into

my gold silk organza dress with gathered straps and a deep 'V' in both front and back, and I'm thankful I do not have the same boobage problem my sister does. I'm almost positive she required industrial strength glue and a prayer to get a bra that worked.

Not three seconds later, Evan pops in with her hair down in waves.

"Nice sex hair, Squirt."

"Dude. I tried. I really did, but..." she gave me a look that said *what are ya gonna do.* I agree. Sex happens when your husband is hot. No harm no foul.

I shrugged and nodded, and then we helped Aurelia into her dress, grabbed our bouquets, and hit the road. Or I should say we traveled to the venue. Man, it's good to have Wraiths around.

The wedding itself was simple and elegant. No random hipster poem readings, no bullshit, no fuss. Just Aurelia and Rhys standing in front of a massive oak tree swathed in thin gauzy fabric and twinkle lights. Aurelia had Henry on her hip, and Rhys had Livy on his and together they held hands and promised each other forever.

KYLE

I spent a rare moment away from my mate when I went to Aurelia and Rhys' wedding. I felt horrible about the shit they'd gone through, but I couldn't exactly call them friends yet. Not when my mate was still laying in a hospital bed refusing to wake up.

I didn't know if Nic would ever open her eyes. I didn't know if there was anything in her that would allow her to come back to me. I missed her. I missed her so much.

I left the wedding just after the ceremony. Just seeing them together with their children after all Iva had put them through made me feel guilty.

There were many things I regretted about the day Aurelia was attacked. I never should have left without the amulet, for one. I never should have let Iva see me, for two. And third, I should have killed Devereux Emerson with a bullet to the brain long before he touched my woman.

But for now, my regrets are all funneled into one. I wish I would have bound her before all this mess. I wish I would have made her mine.

I think this as I play with her graceful fingers. I've seen those tiny little digits play the piano like it was an extension of her body. I've seen her whip a violin into submission. I've seen those pale hands all over my body, always moving, playing, waving—never stopping even in sleep.

I miss their movement.

Just as I think this, the index finger of her left hand twitches. Then, she sits up in her hospital bed like she's rising from a nightmare.

Thankful, I reach for her, but when she sees me, she flinches back. It's then that I notice some serious problems.

One, the Nicola I know is blind. She was born that way.

Two, the Nicola I know has cornflower blue eyes.

This woman can most assuredly see me, and her eyes are an odd honey brown—the same color Iva's were when she took Nic over. I control my rising panic.

"Nicola, sweetheart, it's okay. You're in the hospital, baby," I try and soothe her, holding her hand even as she tries to back away, but she looks confused.

"Th-that's not my name," she says, and with a feeling of dread, I ask the question I'm not sure I want the answer to.

"What *is* your name then?" I ask calmly as I push the nurse call button.

"It's... Well... I-I don't know," she answers frowning at the white hospital blankets.

Wonderful.

Thank you so much for reading Fate Kissed. Evan & West burrowed into my heart and just wouldn't let go. But we aren't quite done yet! Next up is Nicola & Kyle and all the heart wrenching, forbidden mates chaos that is to come.

Shade Kissed is next on the menu, and I hope you're buckled in to see the forgetful, former oracle and her swoony, over-protective mate.

Grab Shade Kissed today!

Want the skinny on future releases without having to follow me absolutely everywhere on social media?
Text "LEGION" to (844) 311-5791

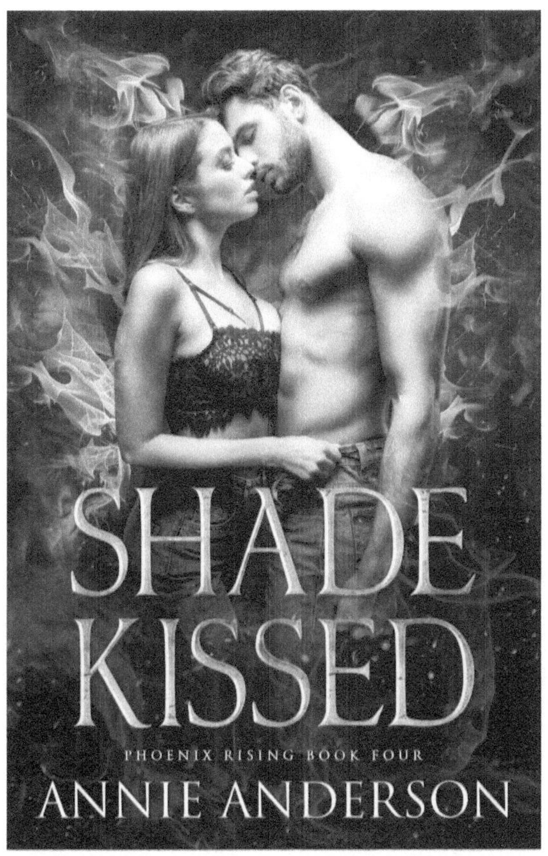

I should have stayed in a coma.

I can't remember a single second of my life before waking up in a hospital bed in Knoxville, Tennessee. Not who I am. Not what I am. Not the man next to me claiming to be my husband.

But the last shards of my life are about to be burned to the ground. Because someone has to pay for the sins of the past, and I'm wearing the face of the woman who committed them.

The old adage is wrong. *What I don't know will definitely kill me.*

NICOLA—AFTER

I come back to myself slowly—painfully—in fits and starts of consciousness. Feeling my heart first, the slow plodding of a body in rest, then the cool stagnant air of a closed room on my skin. The rough but soft bedding surrounding my legs and then the thing that makes my eyes flash open in fear—the warm heat of a hand on mine. I sit up as if I was shot from a cannon, my eyes flashing open for the first time in what feels like a long time.

I can't remember what I'm so afraid of...

My mind trills with the alarm of danger, but I can't place where it's coming from or why. As my eyes scan the dim room, they instantly snag on the form of a man standing next to me. His body is enormous, standing several inches over six feet, his legs encased in dark denim and feet shod in dangerous black boots. His hair, which is trapped beneath the raised hood of his sweater, is not quite black but close enough to be confused for it, matching the thick but groomed beard decorating his jaw. His eyes, which are locked on me, are the color of a decadent milk chocolate. His hands reach for me, and my first feeling is fear—dark and clawing—and I rear back, pressing myself into the pillows of the narrow bed I'm sitting on.

Vaguely, my mind latches onto the fact that this is a hospital, but I'm not sure if I'm right or if this is a dream or if I really am in the danger my heart and mind are screaming at me I'm in.

"Nicola, sweetheart, it's okay. You're in the hospital, baby," his rough voice says soothingly, but I am not soothed. I am nowhere near the realm of soothed. It doesn't matter that this forbidding man has a voice that calls to me. The name he called me doesn't sound right, for one, and as handsome as this man is, I have no idea who he is supposed to be to me. He has to be in the wrong room, right?

Right?

He grabs my hand, gently closing his large fingers over mine, and although the heat of him is nice—almost calming—I don't want this stranger touching me. I don't want him looking at me like this—the wary hesitance on his bearded face is twisting my stomach in knots and the name he called me...

That's not me. That's not my name.

"Th-that's not my name," I tell him as I shake my

head. He has it wrong. The wrong room or wrong woman or something. His face is wrong, his expression is hurt mixed with longing and something worse—fear.

Wrong, wrong, wrong.

"What is your name then?" he asks, his voice calm and controlled as he presses the square orange button on the bedrail. I follow the motion of his hand as he stabs the button, trying to think…

"It's… Well…" I pause, concentrating on a fact which should be so easy to remember, but all I come up with is… *nothing.*

"I-I don't know," I stutter frowning at the white coverlet warming my legs.

I want to say I was holding it together. I want to say my brain went right to denial—which would have helped the situation vastly—that I didn't feel a burning ache in my chest from fear and uncertainty, and Fates knew what else.

But I do—I do feel the ache of loss, of confusion, of unbridled fear.

I don't know my name. How can I not know my name? And who is he? Why is he looking at me like this? What happened to me?

I feel the burn of my breaths coming too fast and my heart pounding too hard. The room begins to spin.

I can't get air... No air... I don't want to go back to the darkness. Nononononononononononono...

The man starts yelling—first at me to breathe and then at the closed door, roaring for help. But his voice is fading, and the room's lights dim further, my sight tunneling to pinpoints. For the life of me, I can't figure out why the fact I'm seeing the light sticks in my mind just before I pass out.

I come to with much less fanfare than the last time. The man isn't there, but a tall, auburn-haired woman is folded in the bedside chair, her eyes closed and her breaths coming in the deep pulls of sleep. Her head is at such an odd angle, resting on her bent, scrub-covered knees as she sleeps curled into an awkward ball in the seat.

I don't want to wake her, but there are a few issues I need to worry about. First, I seem to be attached to this bed by a thick padded cuff on each wrist. This is concerning on so many levels, I'm not sure my brain is taking the time to process it. Second, the original problem of not knowing who I am or where I am or why I'm here is still an issue. A major one. I hate not knowing myself, I hate not knowing how I got here. I clear my throat, realizing too late that at some point I must have been screaming because my throat is on fire.

What the hell happened to me?

The woman comes awake with a start, jumping from her curled ball to her feet with a preternatural grace, her eyes flashing a phosphorescent green. It should worry me. It really should, but for some reason, it doesn't.

"You're not human," I hoarsely croak, stating the obvious. Her lips stretch into a sardonic smile, and it takes her beauty up about ten notches. Her large, almost feline eyes have faded to an odd shade of amber, framed by thick, dark lashes, and she doesn't have a stitch of makeup on her face.

"Neither are you," she returns, her voice a husky alto. This information is not shocking—just like her fantastical jump to her feet, I am not moved. I must have known this before.

Before, I internally scoff. I already hate the word, but I think I need to know a bit more about this 'before' because my brain is not supplying anything other than an extreme lack of shock.

"Are you a healer?" I ask on a wince. What the hell happened to my voice? The woman nods as she pours water into a small blue plastic cup on a rolling bedside table. She eyes my wrists for a moment and plops the pitcher back on the surface with an indelicate thunk.

"My name is Willa, I'm your physician. If I remove your restraints, do you promise not to harm yourself?" she asks with a raised eyebrow. Her eyebrow tells me my answer better be yes, and then her question finally starts to make sense in my head.

I hurt myself? On purpose?

I feel my eyes widen in the surprise I should have had for her jump or her non-human statement, and I quickly nod. Her swift, efficient fingers have my wrists free in mere seconds, but better, her voice prattles on with information. Any and all information is helpful at this point.

"I removed your Foley after your first wake-up call," she says as she moves from my wrists to wave a penlight in front of my eyes. "You've been here for about four months. We weren't sure if you'd ever wake up. Normally, someone of your species should have been up and about ages ago—a week at most, but you're not healing as fast as you should."

Her statement stops me. *I have no idea what I am.*

"Species?" I ask.

"You have no idea, do you?"

"I don't even know my own name, so no, I have absolutely no fucking idea what's going on. Care to share with the class?" I snap. I don't want to snap at her, but I just want to know all of the shit I don't know already.

"Snarky. I like it. I can work with snark, just no more screaming, mmm-kay?"

So this explains what happened to my throat.

"Deal," I reply and Willa holds out the cup as I take a healthy swig. The cool water hits my throat, easing the burn.

"Your name is Nicola. The man who was here before? His name is Kyle. He's your husband."

"Don't start off small, Willa. *Jesus,*" a rumbling voice sounds from the doorway.

The man—Kyle—is in the same clothes as the last time, but his hood has been lowered, giving him a slightly less sinister quality and he now has a pair of thick-framed glasses perched on his nose. His hair is a rumpled mess, as if he has run his hands through it, slept on it, electrocuted himself and possibly took a stroll through a hurricane. He is haggard—probably hasn't slept at all in who knows how long, and imme-diately I want to give him a hug, make him some food and offer the bed to him so he can get some damn rest.

I want to be freaked at the husband comment Willa threw out there like it was no big deal, but I don't think I can be. *Why else would he be here? Why else would he come back? And why do I want to comfort him?*

"Of all the information I need to know, a husband would be at the top of the list, don't you think?" I retort with a shrug.

"You aren't surprised?" Kyle asks.

"I'm finding very few things have surprised me thus far. Can you come in and take a load off? You look like you've been put through the wringer twice."

I get a scowl, a grunted affirmative and a slow shuffle-walk to the bedside chair Willa vacated. In my bones, I know the shuffle is a ruse. He's moving slowly on purpose so I won't freak out. Standing, he has to be closer to seven feet than to six, but I can tell his height and the considerable bulk to his muscles do not hinder his speed in the slightest.

"While all this is well and good, you still haven't told me how I got here or what I am." The question leaves my mouth without thought, and when they exchange a wary glance, I'm not sure I want to know anymore.

NICOLA—NEW ENGLAND 1723

I ran as fast as my little feet could carry me through the brush, stumbling to my hands and knees more times than I could count. Every single day I breathed, I cursed my visions and my sightless eyes, but on days like today, I wished for death more and more.

If I could die—which it seemed I couldn't—I hoped it would be painless, but I had seen death over and over again, and I knew better. Branches whipped my cheeks, stones gouged my feet, but still I ran. Those switches were nothing compared to the danger behind me. He was coming, and he would do horrible things to me when I wouldn't tell him what was to pass.

Didn't he know? I only told death stories, and if death was not to pass, I couldn't tell anyone anything. He'd tried cutting the visions out of me, tried breaking my bones, starving me—but I couldn't tell him what I didn't know.

At first, he called me a devil. Told me I was made of fire and I would bring him death. I'd been drawn to the woman I saw in my vision—not him. She was dying very soon, bound and shackled in a horrific prison where her breaths became more and more labored and her broken body had to fight minute by minute just to keep going. I knew if I were near, she could return to the sky—I could help this good woman start again. I remembered the rites my mother said when papa passed, they were the only good things I remembered about her since she abandoned me in this new place to survive on my own. Every time I saw a good soul die in my visions, I would try to help them move on.

He'd caught me freeing the woman—her body already gone, but her soul was safe now that I'd saved it. He saw my wings, my fire and told me I was of the fallen. When he realized my blindness, he called me Oracle—he said I could tell him his future.

I couldn't. I could only tell him death.

And then the torture started. He must not have had manacles small enough for my eight-year-old wrists—or maybe he did but once he'd starved me for a month, my already thin wrists were able to slip from the irons and I was free.

But not if he caught me.

I felt the air change, the rush of water met my ears just before the fresh, salty smell of the ocean hit my nose. I ran faster until the ground seemed to dip beneath my feet. I tripped again, sliding at breakneck speeds through the rocks toward the sound of crashing waves.

But then cool, slender hands caught me. They weren't his hands—this I knew.

"Do not worry, child. I have come to help you," a woman's voice crooned as she hugged me to her chest.

Her accent was Irish and as soft as a cool summer breeze.

The sound of the man's thrashing through the forest filtered through the trees, and I curled into her, frightened. I didn't want any more of his knives or fists. I didn't want his hot, putrid breath on my face as he called me devil, abomination, demon, harlot. I didn't know what harlot meant, but from his tone, I knew it was bad. I wasn't bad. I was a good girl. I knew I wasn't human, but I couldn't help that. I was born to my strangeness just as I'd been born without sight.

"Cover your ears, child, and I'll take care of this filth," she instructed, calmly brushing my matted hair back from my face. I knew she was going to kill him, and I knew killing was bad, but she was saving me. I couldn't find it in me to care for the man who had tortured me and so many others.

"Wait!" I cried as I clutched to her willowy arm. I didn't want her to leave me. What if she didn't succeed? I needed to have a little piece of her.

"Yes, dearie?" she answered, her voice like watered silk.

"What is your name? I never knew his name. I want to know your name," my voice broke—I was so close to breaking myself.

"My name is Iva, dearie, and I've been looking for you."

Grab Shade Kissed today!

BOOKS BY ANNIE ANDERSON

SEVERED FLAMES

Ruined Wings

IMMORTAL VICES & VIRTUES

HER MONSTROUS MATES

Bury Me

SHADOW SHIFTER BONDS

Shadow Me

THE ARCANE SOULS WORLD

GRAVE TALKER SERIES

Dead to Me

Dead & Gone

Dead Calm

Dead Shift

Dead Ahead

Dead Wrong

Dead & Buried

SOUL READER SERIES

Night Watch

Death Watch

Grave Watch

THE WRONG WITCH SERIES

Spells & Slip-ups

Magic & Mayhem

Errors & Exorcisms

THE LOST WITCH SERIES

Curses & Chaos

Hexes & Hijinx

THE ETHEREAL WORLD

PHOENIX RISING SERIES

(Formerly the Ashes to Ashes Series)

Flame Kissed

Death Kissed

Fate Kissed

Shade Kissed

Sight Kissed

Rogue Ethereal Series

Woman of Blood & Bone

Daughter of Souls & Silence

Lady of Madness & Moonlight

Sister of Embers & Echoes

Priestess of Storms & Stone

Queen of Fate & Fire

To stay up to date on all things Annie Anderson, get exclusive access to ARCs and giveaways, and be a member of a fun, positive, drama-free space, join The Legion!

facebook.com/groups/ThePhoenixLegion

ACKNOWLEDGMENTS

A huge, honking thank you to Shawn, Barb, Jade, Angela, Heather, Kelly, and Erin. Thanks for the late-night calls, the endurance of my whining, the incessant plotting sessions, the wine runs, the trauma I put you through...

Basically, thanks for putting up with my bullshit.

Every single one of you rock and I couldn't have done it without you.

About the Author

Annie Anderson is the author of the international best-selling Rogue Ethereal series. A United States Air Force veteran, Annie pens fast-paced Urban Fantasy novels filled with strong, snarky heroines and a boatload of magic. When she takes a break from writing, she can be found binge-watching The Magicians, flirting with her husband, wrangling children, or bribing her cantankerous dogs to go on a walk.

To find out more about Annie and her books, visit
www.annieande.com

facebook.com/AuthorAnnieAnderson

instagram.com/AnnieAnde

amazon.com/author/annieande

bookbub.com/authors/annie-anderson

goodreads.com/AnnieAnde

pinterest.com/annieande

tiktok.com/@authorannieanderson